He stepped to [...]
didn't have a c [...]

His arm encircled h[...]
him, his mouth dropping to hers.

The kiss took her even more by surprise. It was filled with passion and yearning and possession.

And when it ended, he pulled back to look in her eyes. "Please give me a second chance."

She could do nothing more than nod, her heart a thunder in her chest as he slipped her hand into his large one and they walked across the street like that. She knew the others would be watching from the store-front window, speculating, but she didn't care. His kiss had warmed her all over and his hand felt so good, warm, lightly calloused, strong.

He drove her out to his ranch, touching her cheek or her hand or her arm occasionally on the way as if afraid she might bolt.

B.J. DANIELS

SECOND CHANCE COWBOY

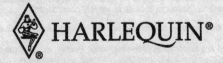
HARLEQUIN®

TORONTO • NEW YORK • LONDON
AMSTERDAM • PARIS • SYDNEY • HAMBURG
STOCKHOLM • ATHENS • TOKYO • MILAN • MADRID
PRAGUE • WARSAW • BUDAPEST • AUCKLAND

Many thanks to my good friend Lynn Kinnaman for not only encouraging me to write this book, but for giving me the ending and making us both cry.

ISBN-13: 978-0-373-69326-9
ISBN-10:   0-373-69326-5

SECOND CHANCE COWBOY

ABOUT THE AUTHOR

B.J. Daniels wrote her first book after a career as an award-winning newspaper journalist and author of 37 published short stories. That first book, *Odd Man Out,* received a 4½ star review from *Romantic Times BOOKreviews* and went on to be nominated for Best Intrigue for that year. Since then she has won numerous awards including a career achievement award for romantic suspense and numerous nominations and awards for best book.

Daniels lives in Montana with her husband, Parker, and two springer spaniels, Spot and Jem. When she isn't writing, she snowboards, camps, boats and plays tennis. Daniels is a member of Mystery Writers of America, Sisters in Crime, Thriller Writers, Kiss of Death and Romance Writers of America.

To contact her, write: B.J. Daniels, P.O. Box 1173, Malta, MT 59538 or e-mail her at bjdaniels@mtintouch.net. Check out her Web page at www.bjdaniels.com.

Books by B.J. Daniels

CAST OF CHARACTERS

Hank Monroe—The former federal agent turned cowboy was running from his past when he was blindsided by the least likely woman of all.

Arlene Evans—The mother of three terrible grown children never dreamed she might get a second chance—let alone a first chance to truly fall in love.

Charlotte Evans—Eighteen, unwed and pregnant, Charlotte thought her worst problem was her mother. But that was before all her lies came back to haunt her.

Meredith Foster—She loved the title Mrs. John Foster more than she loved her husband. But she had no intention of losing either.

John Foster—Trapped in a loveless marriage and a job he hated, he at least thought things couldn't get any worse. But as usual, his wife Meredith surprised him.

Bo Evans—He had his mother buffaloed. As her favorite and the only son, he planned to live off her the rest of his life.

Lucas Bronson—The biker had come home to face his fears. He just hoped he wasn't too late.

Violet Evans—She'd fooled the doctors at the state mental hospital. Now it was only a matter of time before she got out and finished the job she'd started.

The Whitehorse Sewing Circle—This group of women had been meeting for years to run an illegal adoption agency as well as making quilts for every baby born in the area. Today wasn't any different.

Chapter One

Friday, 2:43 p.m.

Charlotte Evans was already late for her doctor's appointment when she looked up and saw a silver SUV blocking the narrow road into town.

The hood of the SUV was up. No sign of the driver.

"Great," Charlotte muttered as she braked to a stop. She should have taken the main road. But, as was her habit, she preferred taking the shortcut into town even though it was more rugged. Normally it was faster. Less chance of getting behind a tractor or a doddering old farmer in a beat-up pickup or cowboys moving a herd of cattle.

She considered turning around. But the barrow pits on both sides of the road were deep and muddy from last night's rain, the road too narrow and steep here above the creek—and, in her condition, an insane idea. There were enough crazy people in her family as it was.

She waited for a moment, motor running. It was one of those hot July days, the Montana sky wide and blue, only a few clouds dotting the horizon. She had her window down, since her old car didn't have air-conditioning. The hot summer air was making her sweat. She hated to sweat.

Still no sign of the driver. She beeped her horn.

A hand waved a hello from under the hood.

"Terrific," Charlotte said under her breath and shut off her engine. How long was this going to take?

It was hard enough living so far from town, let alone getting herself behind the wheel eight months pregnant.

She really didn't need this. To make matters worse, on the way to Whitehorse she'd started having contractions.

It would be just her luck to have this baby beside the road. Somehow that might be fitting, she thought. She just hoped the driver of the SUV knew how to deliver a baby.

Opening her car door, she maneuvered her ungainly belly from behind the steering wheel and got out. She told herself she would never have gotten pregnant if she'd known even half of the things that were going to happen to her body. If only.

Slamming her car door, she waddled toward the SUV, cursing under her breath.

A head appeared as the driver leaned out from the front of the car. "Sorry, didn't hear you drive up," the female driver called. "Had my head stuck under the hood." The head disappeared again.

Charlotte wondered how things could get worse. She just hoped this woman knew what she was doing under there.

At least if the driver had been a man, there might be a chance he could get the car moved out of the way so she could get to town.

She stopped for a moment as another contraction took her breath away. She remembered her doctor saying something about false labor. She hoped that was what this was. Maybe she should have read even one of the books her mother kept buying her about labor and delivery, Lamaze, breast feeding and child rearing.

The last book really was a kick, since her mother had done such a bang-up job with her three, Charlotte thought uncharitably. Actually, being pregnant had made her wonder how her mother had gone through it three times much less raised three kids alone.

As Charlotte waddled the rest of the way up to the front of the SUV, she saw that the woman was teetering on the bumper as she leaned under the hood to work on the engine—wearing a pair of latex gloves, of all things.

"It just quit running," the woman said, looking up. She was at least fifteen years older than Charlotte, with brown hair and eyes and a look of privilege about her. Charlotte would have hated her on sight except that the woman had a smudge of grease on her cheek and she was almost as pregnant as Charlotte herself.

The woman smiled. "Know anything about cars?"

She'd taken an auto mechanics course last year in high school, but she hadn't paid any attention. She shook her head with a silent groan. Apparently this *could* get worse. "Did you call AAA or one of the local garages in town?"

"No cell phone coverage out here."

"I really need to get to my doctor's appointment," Charlotte said. "If we could just move your car over a little, I think I can squeeze mine past. I can drive you into town and you can get someone to come back out with you to work on it."

"I think I've got it fixed. Would you mind getting in and trying to start it while I jiggle this cable?"

Charlotte sighed. Just the thought of trying to climb into the huge SUV— She bent over a little, grimacing as she was hit with another contraction.

The woman was giving her a worried look. "Tell me you aren't in labor."

Charlotte held up her hand and breathed through the contraction. It felt so good when it stopped. "False labor." She hoped.

"How far along are you?" the woman asked, studying her.

"Eight months." The lie came so naturally. "You?"

"Seven. So how close are your contractions?"

Charlotte shrugged. "Not that close."

"Your first baby?"

Charlotte nodded and felt the woman looking at her ring finger. "I'm separated from the father." That was actually kind of true. "I'm older than I look." Another lie.

"Must be difficult. Having a baby all by yourself."

She had her mother and her worthless brother, but she didn't mention that. She knew how pathetic it would sound. Even more pathetic if the woman knew the half of it.

"You can understand why I need to get into town to the doctor," Charlotte said.

"Yes. We definitely need to see to you. But I don't think it's going to be a problem. Just pop behind the wheel and try to start the engine. This should at least allow us to get the car out of the way if nothing else. Neither of us is up to pushing it."

The woman had a point. Although arguing was second nature to Charlotte, who'd been arguing for years. With her older sister. With her mother. With her brother. With herself.

But she wasn't up to it right now, and the woman was right. She didn't want to have to push the SUV out of the way and she doubted she could get past it anyway, as steep and unstable as the edge of the road was.

She opened the door of the pricey SUV and, with great effort, pulled herself up to slide behind the wheel. Her feet were a mile from the gas pedal.

"I need to move the seat forward," she called as she bent over as best she could to look for a handle.

She felt the cool metal the moment it was jammed against her throat.

The pregnant thirtysomething driver of the SUV held a gun in her hand. It was so incongruous: this obviously wealthy pregnant woman with the expensive clothes, salon haircut and freshly manicured nails beneath latex gloves holding a gun on *her.*

It made no sense. That was probably why it didn't register that she was in serious trouble until it was too late.

Chapter Two

At the Whitehorse Sewing Circle, the women gathered around the quilting frame were unusually quiet on this hot summer afternoon.

Normally they would have been abuzz with chatter. Instead they were sipping lemonade, eating the dainty little cookies Laci Cavanaugh had sent over, and smiling a lot—while busting at the seams to share the latest gossip the moment Pearl Cavanaugh left.

Pearl, whose mother had started the group too many years ago for most to remember, had a strict rule about gossip.

But Pearl hadn't been coming for months since her stroke, and the group had taken to gossiping and quilting with a relish. Pearl had been living at the nursing home until recently. Now that she was better and mobile in her wheelchair, Titus had brought her home to stay.

She hadn't quite gotten the knack of sewing with her left hand, but she tried hard. And there wasn't anyone in the group who was going to say she couldn't sew if she wanted to.

To a lot of people Pearl and Titus Cavanaugh were Old Town Whitehorse royalty. Both were feared—if not respected.

"Well, isn't Pearl looking well," said Alice Miller the moment Titus had wheeled his wife out the door.

It wasn't until they heard the crunch of gravel as Titus left with his wife that Helene Merchant gave out a relieved sigh accompanied by a laugh and said, "I thought we were never going to get to visit."

A few of the women laughed with her. Alice Miller, who always sided against gossip, pursed her lips but said nothing. She had tried since Pearl left to keep the women in line, but she was ninety and had given up, saving her energy for quilting.

The problem was, in Old Town Whitehorse there was always something to talk about. Even on a slow day there was always the Evans family.

Old Town was the site of the original Whitehorse. But when the railroad came through five miles to the north, by the Milk River, the town had moved and taken the name with it.

Some of the more hearty homesteaders had stayed in what was now called Old Town. They'd kept the original Whitehorse Cemetery—the name forged in a wrought-iron arch over the entrance—where many of their kin rested for eternity.

The Whitehorse Community Center, the one-room schoolhouse and a few houses were all that was left of the town. Titus Cavanaugh, Pearl's husband, still performed church services at the center on Sundays and took care of hiring a schoolteacher for the school. He was as close to a mayor as Old Town had.

"Have you heard any more about Violet Evans?" Pamela Chambers asked in a whisper, as if the walls had ears.

"That crazy place she's in gave her a job," Helene said. "She's working at a nurses' station. The word is they're going to let her out of the nuthouse and back on the streets. *Doctors*."

"It scares me," Muriel Brown said. "We all know how dangerous she is. Remember the summer all the cats disappeared? Violet always had that look in her eye from the time she was little."

Even Alice Miller couldn't argue the point.

"The other daughter—Charlotte? She's about to have a baby any day," Corky Mathews said. "How old is she anyway?"

"Eighteen, nineteen at the oldest," Helene said. "Anyone heard who was responsible for fathering the baby?"

There was a general shake of heads. This had been a popular topic for months. "Could be anyone," Helene said. "But you know what I heard at the Cut and Curl?"

The women all leaned in. Except for Alice Miller, who sometimes wished her hearing wasn't as good as it was.

"It was some older man from out of town." Helene nodded and went back to her stitching.

"Poor Arlene. You have to feel for her," Muriel said. "Look how her children have turned out. Violet crazy, Charlotte in the family way and Bo, well, is he the most worthless young man you've ever seen? I wonder if Arlene will ever come back to the group."

Looks were exchanged around the table, along with shrugs. Arlene did always have the latest gossip, but with Pearl returning now...

"Eve Bailey's marrying the sheriff," Alice Miller threw in, hoping to give the poor Evans family a break.

The conversation turned to weddings and the possibility of more babies. The Whitehorse Sewing Circle was famous for its quilts. For years the circle had made a quilt for every newborn.

"I saw the cutest pattern," Pamela said, and the afternoon passed in a blur of talk of quilt patterns, material and—always a good standby—food and the latest recipe one of them had tried, as the group stitched away just as it had done for years.

Friday, 6:38 p.m.

ARLENE EVANS STARED at the image in the mirror and felt like crying. She'd changed clothes four times already. If she didn't make up her mind and quickly, she was going to be late. Why had she accepted a date in the first place? She was too old to date.

When Hank Monroe had asked her out, she'd been so excited and surprised she hadn't thought about the actual *date* part. But the reality set in the moment she went to buy something to wear.

For years she hadn't given a thought to the way she looked. No one else had, either. Floyd, her former husband of too many years to count, had hardly given her a sideways glance. So she'd worn what any working ranch woman wore: an oversize long-sleeved Western shirt, jeans and boots. She couldn't remember the last time she'd worn a dress—and she'd bet neither could anyone else in the county.

Her brown hair was long, thick and straight as a stick— the same haircut she'd had in high school, which she trimmed herself when she remembered. Usually her hair was either swept up in a ponytail or thrust under a hat, so she paid little attention to it. She couldn't remember the last time she'd worn her hair down, let alone curled it.

"Stop acting foolish," she snapped at her image in the mirror as she snatched up an elastic band and pulled her drooping curls up into a ponytail.

She took off the dress she'd spent too much money on, tears welling in her eyes as she recalled how cute it had looked on the hanger.

"What did you expect?" she asked herself, sounding just like her mother. Her mother, even dead for years, was right. "Can't make a silk purse out of a sow's ear."

Arlene hurriedly washed the makeup she'd experimented with from her face and changed into a shirt, jeans and boots. She was what she was, and this date with Hank Monroe was a one-time shot.

She thought about the first time she'd seen him and couldn't help but smile. He'd called about signing up for her rural Internet dating service. His voice had been deep and soft and had a strange thrilling effect on her.

They'd agreed to meet at a local café so she could get him signed up. She'd been nervous about meeting him because he wasn't like most of her clients—twenty- to thirtysomething. He was forty-eight—mature, like herself.

The minute she'd walked into the café, she'd spotted him. He'd looked up and their eyes had met.

It sounded ridiculous, she knew, but her heart had begun to pound wildly. Hank Monroe wasn't handsome, but there was a masculine strength in his features and in the broad shoulders, slim hips and long legs cased in denim. He looked like a man who could wrestle grizzly bears if he had a mind to.

And, her smile growing as she remembered the first time he'd laughed, he'd made *her* laugh, surprising them both since hers resembled a donkey's bray.

Hank Monroe had made her feel young and beautiful—all the things she wasn't.

Which should be a clue.

Her mother again. But it was true. Hank had signed up for her dating service to meet *women,* not date the owner of the service. Who knows why he'd asked *her* out? Just being polite, she could only assume, suddenly glad she hadn't dressed up. No reason to act like this was a real date after all.

As she came out of her bedroom, she found her son Bo sitting on the couch, watching television, a huge bag of potato chips in his lap, his bare feet up on her coffee table.

With a frown, she brushed his feet off the table and took the bag of chips from him even as he protested.

"Hey! What am I supposed to eat for dinner?" he groused.

"There are leftovers in the fridge," she said, putting a clip on the chips and taking a cloth back to the living room to wipe the smudges from the coffee table.

"Leftovers?" he demanded indignantly.

She turned down the television volume and straightened to look at her twenty-three-year-old son. He'd been her pride and joy. In her eyes he could do no wrong. She shuddered as she recalled when that had changed.

"Where is your sister?" she asked, determined not to get into an argument with him. Not before her date, anyway.

He shrugged.

Arlene realized she hadn't seen Charlotte since her almost-nineteen-year-old had left for her doctor's appointment earlier that afternoon. Charlotte's old blue sedan wasn't parked out front, and Arlene realized she hadn't heard Bo and Charlotte arguing for hours.

"She should be back from her doctor's appointment by now. Did she call?"

Bo's attention was back on the television. "Nope."

Arlene frowned, hoping the appointment had gone well. Charlotte had been more irritable than usual before she'd left. Arlene remembered how uncomfortable it was being pregnant the last few months. She wondered if Charlotte wasn't having second thoughts about keeping the baby. She could only hope.

"Well, when your sister gets home. make sure she eats something besides potato chips and candy bars. Remind her she's feeding a baby who needs something nutritious to eat."

For a moment Arlene thought about canceling her date. If she didn't cook something, she was afraid neither Bo nor Charlotte would eat properly.

"Promise me you'll eat and make sure Charlotte does."

Bo rolled his eyes. He'd heard this enough times. For months she'd harped on Charlotte to take care of herself for the baby's sake. Not that Charlotte had any business being pregnant, Arlene thought as she headed for her car— and her date.

Her date. What *had* she been thinking? Dating was for

people half her age who still had the stamina—and the optimism. She had neither.

She'd made a point of insisting she would meet Hank Monroe at the restaurant. He'd wanted to pick her up at her house, but the last thing she wanted was for him to meet her family. She knew that once he did, it would be the kiss of death, and she just wanted to enjoy this moment in time knowing it couldn't last anyway.

Why shoot herself in the foot before she even got out of the starting gate?

HANK MONROE LOOKED up as his date came through the restaurant door. He smiled, recalling the first time he'd laid eyes on her. What was it about Arlene that had resonated with his own life? He couldn't be sure. Something in her soft brown eyes. In the determined set of her shoulders. In her hesitant, shy smile.

And that laugh…

Now, as he watched her tug her shirt down over her slim jeans and saw how uncomfortable she looked as she glanced around the restaurant, he felt his heart go out to her again.

Arlene was tall and rangy like a lot of Montana ranch women. Nothing like his petite, classically pretty ex-wife Bitsy. He tried not to see Arlene through Bitsy's eyes. Bitsy took everything at face value. She would never have understood what he saw in this woman. But then, Bitsy had never understood him, had she?

Nor would Bitsy appreciate a woman like Arlene Evans. Few people would, he realized. Bitsy had always been comfortable in her skin. Arlene, he suspected, never had.

He rose quickly, his smile broadening, hoping to

reassure her. "You look wonderful." It was true, although he saw she didn't believe it.

Her cheeks flared. "I didn't know what to wear."

"Your choice was perfect." He pulled out the chair for her and mentally kicked himself. He shouldn't have picked a fancy restaurant for their first date.

As he took the chair across from her, he watched her try to relax. Something else that didn't come easy for Arlene. The woman had an energy that was like being close to a live electrical wire.

"I haven't been on a date in a while," she said.

He smiled. "Me either. Feels odd, huh?"

"Yes. But…nice."

It did feel nice. "So tell me how the matchmaking business is going," he said, leaning toward her.

She brightened and told him she had a half dozen new clients just this week alone. "I still can't believe it."

"You had a great idea and you've made it happen. You should be very proud of yourself."

"Knock on wood," she said, lightly tapping the table.

She didn't seem the superstitious type. He wondered what had her worried. Or if, like him, she was leery when things seemed to be going too well.

LATER THAT NIGHT, after their date, Hank had that exact feeling as he checked the perimeter of the ranch house, as he always did before he entered the house. Old habits died hard. Other people would have thought it paranoid. For him it was merely prudent and part of his life. The life he'd once chosen and had only recently escaped from.

He'd had a great time tonight. That alone worried him.

He'd signed up for the dating service on a whim. Once he'd met Arlene, he hadn't wanted to meet any other women. He wasn't even sure he was ready to date. It felt too dangerous. But he'd asked Arlene out. And he couldn't say he was sorry. Just worried.

There were some things that were inescapable. Guilt. Regret. And his old life. It dwarfed the other two in comparison.

That was the reason he never bothered to lock his house. He knew from experience how easy it was to get into any house, even those with expensive security systems. He had bought the ranch from a corporation that had used the house for conferences.

Because of that, the place was way too large for him. But he'd fallen in love with the view of the Little Rockies and he'd told himself that with all the land surrounding the place he would be as safe here as anywhere.

As he stepped into the house, he found himself whistling. He couldn't remember a night he'd enjoyed more. Arlene was a fun date—once she relaxed.

They'd had dinner, then gone to the movie—the only one in Whitehorse. A comedy had been showing. That was something else he had in common with Arlene—the way they laughed.

"You bray like a donkey," Bitsy had told him when they'd first gotten together. "You really need to do something about that."

He'd quit laughing around her.

During the movie, he'd found himself simply enjoying the sound of Arlene's laugh. It had felt so good, so natural.

Later, he'd thought about kissing her good-night but

had chickened out. *Coward*. The desire had been there. He'd told himself he was just afraid of scaring her off. Clearly this dating thing was as alien to her as it was to him.

But he knew that he was the one who wanted to take it slow. That was another thing they shared—the feeling that when things were going too well, something was bound to happen to jinx it.

As he passed his office, he saw that the message light on his answering machine was flashing. He preferred an answering machine with small disposable tapes over voice mail. Just as he'd always periodically checked his house and car for listening devices. Even here on the ranch in Montana.

He would have liked to believe he'd dropped off his former associates' radar. But he'd worked for the agency too long to pretend that was even possible.

Still, as he pushed the play button, he was startled to hear a familiar voice.

"Hank, it's Cameron. Call me. We need to catch up. It's been too long."

He stared down at the machine, shaken. By the unexpected sound of his old friend and former boss's voice as much as by the calmness of the words—and the underlying threat. Code words. They brought it all back, and for a moment it was as if he'd never left the agency.

He didn't need to replay the message. He quickly deleted it, knowing it was futile to think that would be the end of it. The words echoed in his head. Code words that informed him there's been a breach in security. He was in danger.

ARLENE EVANS WOKE smiling. That alone shocked her. Normally the blare of Bo's music down the hall or the sound of Charlotte clamoring around in the kitchen started her day off wrong.

But this morning, after her date with Hank Monroe, nothing could ruin her good mood. They'd had a nice dinner. He'd been easy to talk to. The movie had been enjoyable. They'd stood out in the moonlight and talked afterward.

She been afraid he'd kiss her. And afraid he wouldn't. He didn't. But he'd asked her out again. She felt like a schoolgirl.

Just the thought seemed…foolish. She was too old to be having these feelings. Especially the ones Hank Monroe had sparked with just the brush of his fingers when they'd both reached for the popcorn at the same time. Or when he'd put his arm around her. Or touched her back with the palm of his hand as they'd left the theater. Desire after all these years of feeling nothing?

She rose and dressed, wrapped in the memory of the night before and the prospect of another date tonight. He'd also invited her to the county fair this coming weekend—his first county fair, he'd said.

She hadn't told him, but she planned to enter in the baking division and almost always took blue ribbons. It was the one thing she excelled in, and normally she would be a nervous wreck worrying that she might not win this year. That she'd lost her touch.

But Hank Monroe had taken her mind off the fair this year.

Which, she reminded herself sternly, wasn't good.

Baking lasted. Men didn't. "Stick to what you're good at," her mother had always said. "It's little enough."

Arlene felt her smile slip. She was making too much of one date with the man. Getting her hopes up was always a mistake.

She'd learned that the hard way, she thought, remembering high school dates that never showed while she waited by the window and her mother berated her for opening herself up to that kind of humiliation.

By the time Arlene reached the kitchen, she was no longer smiling. She yelled down the hall for Bo to turn down the music. He didn't. She started to tell Charlotte to go down the hall and tell him when she noticed her daughter wasn't lying on the couch, where she usually was this time of the morning. Nor was the television on or the kitchen counter a mess from where Charlotte had made herself a snack before breakfast.

More puzzled than worried, Arlene walked down the hall to her daughter's bedroom and pushed open the door. The bed was just as it had been when Arlene made it the previous morning.

Charlotte hadn't come home last night.

Stepping across the hall, she opened her son's bedroom door. The room was bedlam—just the way he apparently liked it. He'd barred her from cleaning it, which she should have been grateful for. Instead the room was an embarrassment, a reflection on her.

"What if someone comes by and sees this mess?" she'd demanded time after time.

"No one comes by," he'd said.

"Well, if anyone did, they'd think I was a terrible mother."

Bo had laughed at that.

"Have you seen your sister?" she mouthed now over the horrible music blasting from his stereo.

He was sprawled on his bed, frowning at her and motioning for her to go away and close the door.

She reached over and grabbed the cord on the stereo and pulled hard. The music stopped, filling the room with an abrupt deafening silence.

"What?" he demanded.

"Your sister. She didn't come home last night."

"So?"

"She's eight months pregnant."

"I noticed. But I'm not my sister's keeper." He reached to plug the stereo back in, but she still held the cord and jerked it back out of his grasp.

"I want you to clean your room."

He looked at her as if she'd lost her mind.

"I'm serious, Bo."

He mugged a face at her.

"I also want you to get a job."

He let out a surprised laugh. "I have a job. I help you with your Internet dating service."

"No, you don't." She tossed him the end of the cord and closed the door behind her, telling herself she shouldn't be worried about Charlotte.

Actually, this was just like her daughter. Charlotte had been cranky yesterday and late for her doctor's appointment. Arlene had tried to talk to her again about putting the baby up for adoption. Charlotte hadn't come home just to punish her.

Arlene told herself she wasn't going to rise to Charlotte's

bait. Not this time. But she worried about the baby. That poor, innocent baby was going to need a mother—and soon.

The phone rang. "Hello." She just assumed it would be Charlotte making ultimatums before she came home.

"Arlene?"

Just the sound of Hank Monroe's deep voice buoyed her spirits instantly. "Hank," she said a little breathlessly.

"Is everything all right?"

"Fine," she said too cheerfully, hoping he didn't hear the slight catch in her throat.

"Arlene, you can be honest with me. What's wrong?"

She took a deep breath and let it out slowly. He was going to find out sooner or later anyway. Wouldn't it be better if it came from her? "It's my daughter. My youngest daughter. She's pregnant. Not married. And she didn't come home last night."

"Maybe she's with her boyfriend."

"I don't think there *is* a boyfriend. At least not one who's free."

"I see," he said. "How about her friends? Have you tried them?"

"She doesn't have a lot in common with her old friends anymore." Arlene felt her throat close and fought back the tears. Most of the time she could stand what her life had become. But revealing the truth to Hank made it more real, more sad and tragic.

"I was just getting ready to call the doctor's office and see if anything unusual happened during her visit yesterday."

"All right. Let me know what you find out."

She promised she would and called the doctor's office, only to get a recording. It was too early. She'd have to wait.

And the one thing she really wasn't good at was waiting. Grabbing her purse, she headed for the door.

THE MOMENT SHE walked into the sheriff's office Arlene knew it was a mistake.

"Arlene," Sheriff Carter Jackson said as he got to his feet. He didn't look happy to see her. But then, who could blame him given the other times she'd come in raging in defense of her children over whatever trouble they'd gotten into?

"It's Charlotte," she said, hating that her voice broke. She always tried so hard to be strong, believing a woman alone had to be strong or the world would crush her in an instant. "She's missing."

"Missing," he repeated, then motioned to the chair opposite his desk as he dropped back into his. "When was the last time you saw her?"

Arlene took the chair but teetered on the edge, too nervous to relax. She hated being forced to come here.

"Yesterday afternoon, when she left for her doctor's appointment. She didn't come home last night and she never made her doctor's appointment. I just stopped by the doctor's house. No one has seen her."

He leaned back in his chair and rubbed his jaw as he studied her. "Is it possible she's run away?"

"No. I mean, I can't imagine. She's eight months pregnant."

He nodded. "Maybe she left with the baby's father."

Arlene felt sick. "I think he's married."

The sheriff picked up his pen and tapped it on a stack of papers on his desk. "You realize I can't file a missing-persons report until she's been gone for at least twenty-four hours, but I'll tell the deputies to keep an eye out for her."

"I'm afraid something has happened to her."

"I can understand your concern."

"Can you?" She hated the edge to her voice.

"I'll admit, Arlene, that I can't help but be skeptical. It isn't like we haven't been here before."

She rose. "Well, thank you for your time," she said, turning and stiffening her back, head high, as she headed for the door.

"Keep me apprised of the situation," he called after her. "I'm sure you'll hear from her soon."

As she left, fighting tears of frustration, she passed Eve Bailey coming in. She hadn't seen her neighbor for a while and was surprised how happy Eve looked, then recalled that Eve and the sheriff were to be married in the coming week.

Arlene nodded at Eve as they passed, not trusting her voice. She'd always wanted that for her daughters. A handsome, eligible man. A wedding where everyone in the county came to celebrate. A white wedding dress and the mother-daughter talk.

She'd wanted that desperately because she'd never had it.

She fought the tears all the way to her pickup. What had she done wrong? At the rate things were going, she'd never have to worry about buying a mother-of-the-bride dress or fussing over last-minute details with the caterer.

Eve Bailey wasn't getting cold feet. She was marrying the man she loved—had loved since she was a girl.

But now that the Fourth of July was coming up so quickly, she was anxious. She wanted this wedding to be perfect.

Her mother, with her new husband Loren Jackson, would be flying in. Her father, Chester Bailey, would be giving her away. He would be attending the wedding with his girlfriend Susie.

How did other families handle all this extended-family stuff? She just hoped there wouldn't be any trouble. But that wasn't what bothered her. Here she was with all this extra family and she wasn't related by blood to any of them except for her twin, Bridger Duvall.

She had hoped by the time she married Sheriff Carter Jackson that she would know who she was. For years she'd yearned for someone who looked like her. Bridger had her coloring, but it wasn't like being able to look at your mother and father and see yourself.

She had tried to accept that she would never have that because of the circumstances of her adoption. But still she wondered what her birth mother was like. Was she even still alive? On her wedding day, Eve would have loved to have her "other" family in the pews as well as her adopted family.

Unfortunately she and her adoptive mother had never been close. Eve blamed herself. She knew she had been a difficult child. From early on she'd known Lila wasn't her "real" mother even though Lila had sworn differently. It didn't seem to matter that Lila loved her and considered Eve her own.

Eve hoped to make up for that somehow. But looking for her birth mother had only made the chasm between her and Lila grow wider—and brought light to the illegal adoption ring.

"Is everything all right?" Carter asked as she stopped in his office doorway, hands on her slim hips, dressed in

Western attire with a straw hat pulled low over her long dark hair.

"Yes. No. I think so."

He laughed and came around his desk to take her in his arms. "Just a little longer," he whispered against her ear.

She nodded, sick of thinking about nothing but the wedding. "Was that Arlene Evans I just saw leaving? She looked different somehow."

"Charlotte seems to be missing," he said as he motioned Eve into a chair and took one opposite her.

"The girl is about to have a baby any day, isn't she?"

He nodded.

"Poor Arlene, those kids have put her through hell," Eve said. "What if our kids turn out like that?"

"I'll lock them up down here in the cells until they straighten up."

Her eyes widened even though she knew he was kidding. "Seriously, there could be some bad gene in Bridger's and my blood that we don't know about."

Carter's face softened. "There is no bad gene. Look how well both of you turned out."

"Right." But Eve couldn't help but worry. Soon they would be having children. The sooner, the better, since she was now thirty-four. At least their kids would be able to look at their parents and know who they were, even though their mother still probably wouldn't have a clue who she was or where she'd come from.

"I'm okay," she said, seeing the worry in her soon-to-be husband's face. "Really. It's just the wedding and everything." She reached across to squeeze his hand.

She had one constant she could hang on to: she knew

she belonged with Sheriff Carter Jackson. Now, if they could just get through the wedding without anything like sheriff business keeping him from the altar…

As ARLENE CLIMBED behind the wheel of her pickup, she didn't blame Sheriff Carter Jackson for being skeptical about Charlotte's disappearing act. Arlene herself couldn't help but believe he might be right.

She blamed herself. She'd failed miserably as a mother. It was the only explanation for the way her three had turned out. And even now she had no idea what she'd done wrong. Floyd had always been too busy farming— until recently, when he'd bailed out completely.

Drying her tears, she pulled herself together as she drove home. She had to believe that Charlotte would come back and that that innocent little baby was all right.

"Arlene?" Hank's voice sounded like heaven when he answered the phone. "Any news on your daughter?"

She swallowed the lump in her throat and turned her back to Bo, who was sprawled on the couch, watching television. "She never went to her doctor's appointment yesterday, and I still haven't heard a word. I'm worried sick."

"I'll come right out and help you look for her."

She glanced over her shoulder at Bo. "I don't think that's a good idea."

"Arlene, I want to help."

She'd hoped to put this off. She took the phone outside to the porch and closed the door firmly behind her.

"The truth is, I haven't been honest with you about my family." The tears that burned her eyes surprised her. She hadn't cried for years, and now all of a sudden she was a waterworks. "I've made a horrible mess of my life. Of my children's lives. I have one daughter in a mental institution, another one pregnant and a son—" Her voice broke and she couldn't continue.

"I haven't told you about my family either," Hank said. "I've made my share of mistakes, as well, Arlene. You know I told you I was widowed? It's true. My wife and I never divorced but we hadn't lived together for years. I'm walking out the door now. I can be at your place in fifteen minutes. Just give me the directions. We'll find your daughter."

Arlene cupped her hand over her mouth for a moment to keep from sobbing, her relief overwhelming her. She'd been handling things on her own for so many years, just the thought of someone wanting to help her… When there were problems, Floyd had always left it up to her to take care of them, blaming her no matter what the trouble was or the outcome.

"You need to drive south toward Old Town," she finally managed to say.

"I'll be right there."

Chapter Three

Hank drove down the narrow dirt road, flying over the small rises, dropping down to creek bottoms and cattle crossings.

He hadn't seen another vehicle since he'd left White-horse. Nor was there a house or fence in sight. The land rolled in waves of green grasses toward the badlands of the Missouri Breaks.

Of all the places he'd been in the world, none seemed as desolate as this right now. He'd heard this called one of the loneliest places in America. One hundred and fifty miles of country with only a few roads, none of them passable when wet, scores of townships without a town or even a house and, ripping a deep, twisted canyon through it all was the Missouri River, where the badlands rose up from the canyon floor in pre-glacial cliffs.

This country of purple-shadowed coulees filled with stands of scrub pine, spruce and cedar was what had brought him here. The river bottom was cloaked in thick stands of cottonwoods that reached for the big sky, and the prairie let him see for miles.

Montana was said to have a population density of six people per square mile. Out here that number dropped to zero-point-three people.

He had yearned for isolation. For open spaces. For freedom. Here in this part of Montana, one of the last lawless places, he had found it.

Had he blinked, he would have missed Old Town Whitehorse. A weathered sign was barely visible in the tall weeds beside the road. Whitehorse. Someone had added *Old Town* above the faded lettering in black paint.

Hank slowed as he passed a one-room schoolhouse, the Whitehorse Community Center, a few more old houses, the cemetery with its wrought-iron arch.

The railroad might have lured the first residents to the north, but a lot of Whitehorse apparently had remained right here.

He turned down the road as Arlene had instructed. Not far along he spotted the farmhouse. It was big and white with a wide screened-in porch. Behind it, a faded red barn with a horse weather vane that moved restlessly in the breeze.

He pulled in, parked. As he got out of his SUV, he saw Arlene waiting for him, on the front porch. Her face lit at the sight of him and he felt that pull inside him, his heart beating a little faster, the sky a little bluer.

What was it about this woman? She was far from beautiful. But there was a strength to her. An inner beauty that seemed to radiate from her face when he looked at her.

His grandmother would have said she came from good stock. A woman who'd never been pampered. A woman who he suspected had never been loved—at least not enough. And that, he thought, explained the vulnerability that she tried so hard to hide.

After the phone call from Cameron last night, he knew he shouldn't be here. He didn't want to bring his old life anywhere near this woman, who he suspected had enough problems without him becoming one of them.

But as he walked toward her and saw the determined set of her shoulders under the oversize shirt, the way she stood in boots and slim jeans that emphasized her height, there wasn't a chance in hell that he could turn his back on her.

He'd help her find her daughter, then he'd make some excuse not to see her anymore until he knew what the hell Cameron wanted. A breach in security? That had nothing to do with him any longer. Even if his former enemies had learned who he was, he'd suspected long before he'd quit that all the bad guys knew the other bad guys. That's why he hadn't returned the call. He didn't want any more to do with that spook stuff.

"I shouldn't have called you," Arlene said, coming down the porch steps toward him. "I'm sure this is just Charlotte being Charlotte. I don't want you bothered with it. She likes to worry me."

He smiled ruefully, thinking of his own daughter. "Kids do that."

"Really, I shouldn't have involved you in this," she said nervously.

"Arlene, I want to help. I wouldn't have offered if I didn't."

Tears welled in her eyes. She made a swipe at them. "I made some lemonade."

He didn't need any lemonade, but he had a feeling she needed to keep busy. "Lemonade sounds wonderful."

She glanced toward the house. "My son is home."

"I look forward to meeting him."

Her skeptical glance almost made him laugh as she angled back up onto the porch to open the front door.

He followed her inside. The place was immaculate right down to the plastic covers on the couch and chairs. The floors looked freshly scrubbed, and there wasn't even a dust mote in the air.

The only thing out of place was the young man sprawled on the couch watching TV. He frowned when he saw Hank but didn't move.

"Bo, this is Hank Monroe," she said, biting off each word as she gave a jerk of her head that indicated her son should stand.

Bo ignored the gesture. "So you're dating my mom?" he asked, his tone incredulous as he gave Hank the once-over.

"*Bo,*" Arlene snapped as she stepped into the living room to shut off the television.

Hank said nothing, his gaze locking with Bo's. Bo looked away first, and Hank followed Arlene into the kitchen. He heard the television come back on, but Bo turned it down, obviously not wanting to miss what was going on in the adjacent room.

"I did teach him manners. He just refuses to use them. I'm sorry," Arlene said as she poured Hank a glass of lemonade from a sweating glass pitcher.

"Don't be." He took a sip. The lemonade was wonderful and he said as much.

She beamed and offered him some gingersnaps she'd made. "They take first place at the fair every year." She glanced toward the living room, clearly anxious.

Hank motioned to the chair across from him. "Why don't you tell me when you last saw Charlotte."

Arlene pulled out the chair, brushing at nonexistent crumbs on the seat, and sat down. She took a deep breath and let it out slowly. "I saw her just before she left for her doctor's appointment. Her appointment was for three, but as usual she was running late. I was worried about her driving too fast on the road into Whitehorse. I offered to take her, but…" Her voice broke.

"You said you talked to the doctor and she didn't make her appointment?"

Arlene nodded.

"Had she missed an appointment before?" he asked, pretty sure he already knew the answer.

"Yes, but she was getting so close to her due date I can't imagine her just blowing this one off."

"Okay. There is only one road into Whitehorse, right?"

Arlene's eyes widened as she shifted her gaze to the living room. Bo was caught watching them and instantly got a don't-look-at-me expression.

"Charlotte wouldn't have taken the shortcut would she?" Arlene asked her son.

"Why do you keep asking me what Charlotte would do?" Bo demanded, raising his voice. "I have no idea. It's not like we ever talk. You should know that."

"I should know a lot of things," Arlene snapped.

Bo shot to his feet, angrily snapped off the television and stalked down the hallway. A door slammed, and a few moments later Hank heard a stereo come on.

"Can you show me this shortcut?" Hank said, getting to his feet.

She glanced down the hallway for a moment, and he could see how badly she wanted to go down there and yell at her son. Slowly her gaze came back to him and she rose from her chair as if she was an old woman. Her children were killing her, he thought as they went outside to his vehicle.

"What was Charlotte driving?" he asked.

"A small, dark blue Chevy. I can't remember what year. It's an older-model sedan."

He nodded. "And what was she wearing?"

Arlene shook her head. "I don't remember exactly. She's so big and she refuses to wear maternity clothes, so whatever she had on was stretched over her stomach."

"I think that's the style now."

Arlene looked mystified by that.

"What about the baby's father?" he asked. "Is it possible she's with him?"

"I doubt it. She wouldn't tell me who the man is, but from what I could gather he's involved with someone else. I'm not even sure he knows about the baby."

Hank took that in, wondering how the man couldn't know in a town the size of Whitehorse. From what little time he'd lived in the county he'd discovered there were no secrets. Everyone seemed to know his name even though he spent little time in town and had met only a few people.

"I tried her cell phone," Arlene was saying. "It goes straight to voice mail. I left a message…."

"Maybe you should call the sheriff," he suggested as they drove out of town.

"No." She softened her expression and her words as she continued. "I already spoke to the sheriff. He can't file a missing-persons report yet. The thing is, Charlotte has had some problems with the law. The sheriff thinks this is just one of her stunts—and, you know, he's probably right."

THE SHORTCUT WAS narrow, with deep barrow pits on each side—much like the main road to Old Town Whitehorse.

But the road was closer to the Evans' farmhouse, and since Hank hadn't seen Charlotte's car on his way to Arlene's, this would be the next place to check.

He found himself taking in the land that ran toward the Missouri Breaks, fascinated this untamed country was right out Arlene's back door. Who couldn't get lost in this?

"I'm sure Charlotte probably just stayed in town," Arlene said, drumming her fingers on the armrest. "It's just that I can't imagine who she might have stayed with." When she looked at him, he saw the pain.

He realized he had never known the names of his daughter's friends. There'd been a stream of them in and out of the house over the years, but he'd never been home enough to keep track of them.

His daughter had grown up without him being around. He'd told himself that she was fine, Bitsy was doing a great job raising her. That he wasn't needed. His job was to provide for his family. Only now could he admit what bull that had been.

"What was your husband like?" he asked.

"Absent," she said and craned her neck to look out as the road dipped down to a creek crowded with thick stands of chokecherries and dogwood. "Wait. Back up. I think I saw something."

He stopped the SUV and reversed back up the hill.

"There!" she cried.

He pulled over to the edge of the road as best he could although it wasn't wide enough for another car to pass and put on the emergency flashers even though he doubted any other cars would be coming along. Arlene was already out of the car and running to the edge of the road.

He joined her as she pointed down the slope and saw the patch of blue through the dense, tall brush along the creek.

Closer, he could see the tracks in the soft earth where a car had gone off, some of the sagebrush limbs broken or uprooted.

"Oh, God," Arlene said beside him. She took a step toward the ravine, but he stopped her.

"Stay here. I'll go check."

Arlene looked stricken. "If she went off the road… The baby—"

"Let's not jump to conclusions before we know if that's even her car down there, okay?"

She nodded, although they both knew it had to be.

He walked down the road to a spot where the slope wasn't so steep and worked his way down to where he'd seen the patch of blue from above.

The chokecherries and dogwood were thick and hard to navigate, but he hadn't gone far when he caught the glint of a chrome bumper.

Forcing his way closer, he glanced into the rear window. The car was covered in dust but he could see that there was no one in the backseat.

Working his way along the passenger side of the car,

he covered his hand with the tail of his shirt to open the door. If this was a crime scene, he didn't want to destroy any more evidence than necessary.

The door opened and he peered in. No eight-months-pregnant woman inside. The keys were in the ignition, he noted. The car appeared to be in Neutral.

He glanced around. No sign of a struggle. No blood. No indication anything had been taken, since there were a couple dollars in change in the drink holder and the glove box was still closed.

He glanced at the driver-side door. It was closed, a dense wall of brush against it—just as there had been against the passenger-side door. Just to be sure the car was Charlotte's, he checked the registration in the glove box.

Then, reaching across, he pulled on the trunk lever. The lid groaned open.

Closing the door, he straightened and moved to the rear of the car. He was relieved to find the trunk empty except for the usual junk most people carried there.

He closed the lid, careful not to leave his prints.

"Hank?" Arlene called down, sounding scared.

"She's not here," he called back. "I'll be right up." He climbed out of the ravine to find her standing on the road where he'd left her. She'd worn a path in the dirt, though, where she had paced.

"It's her car, isn't it?"

He nodded. "But she wasn't in it when the car went off the road."

She didn't seem to hear him. "Oh, my God, she could be out there anywhere, wandering around, maybe having her baby."

"Arlene." He touched her arm. "She *wasn't* in the car when it went off the road."

She stared at him. *"What?"*

"Come here." He walked her over to the spot where the car tracks left the road. "See. Someone walked around here, then walked to the edge of the road. See how deep the footprints are?"

"What are you saying?"

"The car was pushed off the road. The keys were in it and the car was in Neutral."

"Why would Charlotte do that?"

"The prints would indicate the size and shape of a woman's shoe."

Arlene met his gaze. "How do you know so much about this kind of stuff?"

"I like murder mysteries," he said truthfully.

She looked sickened as she glanced back down into the ravine. "She's run off, hasn't she?"

"It would appear that way. Her purse isn't in the car. There was no sign of a struggle. Did she take a suitcase or an overnight bag when she left for her doctor's appointment?"

Arlene shook her head. "I don't know. She could have put one in the car the night before."

"We'll know more once we get the car out of the ravine. Who should I call?" He pulled out his cell phone but quickly realized he couldn't get any coverage out here. "I'll call from town."

She nodded and gave him a name of a tow truck operator. "Thank you."

He wished there was something he could say to relieve her worry. "She isn't alone. Someone met her here." He pointed to another set of tire tracks on the opposite side of the road.

"I can't imagine who it could have been." She frowned as if she remembered something.

"What?"

"Just that I've seen a car I didn't recognize drive by the house numerous times over the past few months," she said. "A silver SUV."

"Did you happen to notice the license plate?"

She shook her head. "I didn't pay much attention to it. I wouldn't have noticed it at all except that we get so little traffic out our way."

"You didn't see the driver?"

"No. I can't be sure if it was a man or a woman."

"You don't know of anyone who drives a car like it?" he asked.

She shook her head again. "I wish I was of more help."

"Don't worry. She'll turn up."

"Only if she wants to be found. You don't know Charlotte."

Hank smiled and put his arm around Arlene as he walked her back to his car. "Charlotte doesn't know me."

HANK WAITED UNTIL the tow truck operator unhooked Charlotte's car in the front yard of the farmhouse before opening the car.

Arlene came out of the house and stood on the porch, watching.

Hank slid behind the wheel, careful not to touch anything. He heard Arlene come up to the side of the car.

"You still aren't convinced she ran away," Arlene said.

"Better to be safe than sorry," he said as he tilted his head to study the steering wheel. "How tall did you say your daughter was?"

"Five-four."

"Someone taller drove her car last," he said. "She work on her own car?"

Arlene's laugh had an edge to it. "And ruin her nails?"

He sniffed the steering wheel, then got out and checked the hood latch.

"What is it?" she asked.

"Engine grease on the steering wheel. Whoever drove the car had it on their hands, but it apparently didn't come from this car."

"So it came from the other car," Bo said, coming out of the house to join them. "You already suspected she met someone out there and rode with them. So what's the big deal about the engine grease?"

"Nothing maybe," Hank said. "I guess it would depend on who picked her up out there."

"Seems pretty clear to me," Bo said. "No one uses that shortcut, so it couldn't have been just someone passing by. Charlotte had obviously set it up. No one would see her get into the other car. Seems to me she was buying time by ditching hers." He looked at his mother as if she was the reason Charlotte had run away.

"That's one theory," Hank admitted. "So who *did* pick her up?"

"Don't look at me," Bo said. "I don't know anything about it." He turned to head back into the house.

"But you know who fathered her baby," Hank said to the young man's retreating back.

It was only a slight movement of the shoulders, a telltale sign. "What does it matter anyway? The guy obviously doesn't want anything to do with her."

Arlene looked as if she wanted to trail after her son. "Bo doesn't know anything. He's just talking."

Bo *knew* something. And if he knew, then Hank figured it wouldn't be that hard to find out. There was nothing Hank loved more than a challenge. "I'll see if I can find anything out."

"I've tried for months without any luck."

"Don't worry," he said, giving her a reassuring smile. "I have a way with people."

ARLENE RETURNED his smile, thinking he certainly did. She'd tried for months to find out who the father of the baby was without any luck at all. "I'm not sure it's going to do any good, though. If she's run off with him…"

"Then at least you'll know who she's with."

"Why are you doing this?" she had to ask.

Hank moved to her and took both of her hands in his. "Because I like you and you need help."

She tried to pull away, hating the fact that she needed anyone's help but maybe especially Hank's. That wasn't the relationship she wanted with him. "I don't want you dragged into my problems."

"Arlene, this doesn't change how I feel about you."

How could it not? And how *did* he feel about her? "I'm a terrible mother."

He laughed. "No, you're not."

"Oh, you have no idea. The mistakes I've made…"

"Believe me, my mistakes are legendary."

"I wish I could do it over," she said with heat. "I would do things so differently."

He chuckled. "Wouldn't we all." He let go of her hands to step to the car. She watched him lock it. "For the time being, don't drive the car. Let me see what I can find out."

She nodded numbly. She couldn't help being worried about Charlotte and the baby. "I didn't realize how much I wanted to be there when my first grandbaby was born. I had wanted Charlotte to put the baby up for adoption. But still I thought I could be there for my daughter and at least see the baby…."

She turned away, not wanting him to see her cry. Hank's kindness had turned her into a fountain.

This wasn't the way she'd wanted things to be between them. She didn't want him to know this side of her. Not the woman with all this baggage. How could he even stand to look at her?

"Arlene," he said.

She turned to find him directly behind her.

He cupped her cheek. His thumb pad brushed the corner of her mouth. "Try not to worry," he said softly. "I'll see you tonight."

She looked into his eyes. He still wanted to go out with her tonight? She nodded numbly.

He smiled. "Leave it to me."

She watched him walk to his vehicle, still stunned not only that he'd come into her life, but also that he was still there.

Won't be for long.

Her mother's voice. But Arlene didn't argue with the sentiment. Wait until Hank learned about her daughter Violet.

VIOLET EVANS PEERED out the hospital window, past the pathetic array of patients, to the fence that had become her prison.

Just a few more weeks.

It had been her mantra for months, and lately it hadn't been working—and that worried her more than she wanted to admit.

She'd been doing so well, pretending for months to be catatonic before miraculously coming out of it with no apparent memory of the bad things she'd done in the past. How many people could pull something like that off? Very few if any, she would wager.

She'd always known she was smart, but lately she'd come to realize she might be a genius.

Of course, she had to hide that fact from the doctors. Clearly they weren't half as intelligent as she was, since they had no idea what she was up to.

Just a few more weeks.

And she would be free.

So why couldn't she relax and just do what they were asking of her? Why did she feel as if her insides were starting to show through her skin?

The doctors had insisted she do an in-patient work program to prepare her for when she got out. Which meant she filed for hours at the nurses' station. She thought she would go crazy for sure if she had to do it much longer.

And then there were the nightmares. She'd never told anyone about them. These doctors would have a field day with even one of her dreams. She shuddered to think of what they would make of them. What she herself made of them if she let herself delve too deeply.

Just a few more weeks.

But it was getting harder and harder to remember that, and just the thought of never getting out of here—

She shoved that thought away and concentrated on revenge. But even the revenge she'd planned against her mother had lost some of its power.

Maybe worse than the nightmares was the voice she kept hearing in her head. She'd thought it was her mother's but lately she couldn't be sure it wasn't her grandmother's.

It was distracting and confusing, and she wasn't sure how much longer she could keep this up. The place was literally driving her crazy, making her question things.

Like her mother's culpability in all this.

She shook her head, trying to banish the confusion. Of course it was her mother's fault. Everything was always the mother's fault.

Chapter Four

Bo Evans disliked Hank Monroe even before he'd met the man. He would have disliked any man his mother dated. Not that he felt any loyalty to his father. Floyd Evans was a spineless bastard who'd abandoned them the moment there was trouble. Hell, Floyd Evans had abandoned them long before that.

"What did I tell you?"

He looked up to find his mother standing in front of him. She had the remote in her hand. He swore as she muted his show. "Tell me about what?"

"Getting a job."

He shook his head. It had just been a threat. At least he hoped that's all it had been. "If I got a job, I'd have to be in town all day. Maybe even have to work nights. You'd be here by yourself. You don't want that. You need me around."

His mother laughed and he realized this was a new reaction. "Nice try. I want you to find a job. And then I want you to find a place to live."

He stared at her as if he'd never seen her before. He suspected he hadn't. This was Hank Monroe's doing, the bastard. He'd put this into her head.

"This is about Hank, isn't it? You think he's going to always be around?" Bo scoffed at that. "Once he gets what he's after, he'll be gone. The guy's playing you. He's going to break your heart."

"Well, I've been played before and certainly had my heart broken by those closest to me, haven't I?" she said, shutting off the television. "You have until the end of the week."

"And then what?" he demanded. "You're not going to put me out on the street. Not your favorite son."

To his surprise, she said nothing. Instead she walked over to the garbage can and dropped the remote into it.

Bo told himself she was bluffing, that she was just upset about Charlotte. Once Charlotte was back here and the baby was born, things would get back to normal. Well, as normal as life here had ever been.

"What's the point of throwing away the remote?" he called after her as she headed for her bedroom down the hall.

"Don't worry, you won't need it," she said, stopping to look back at him. "You'll be at work. Anyway, I've had the cable service canceled. Out here we might be able to get *one* of the local stations clear enough for you to watch. So you won't need the remote, because what would be the point of changing the station?" Without another word, she turned and continued to her bedroom, closing the door behind her.

Bo swore and kicked the coffee table over. The one thing he didn't want was anything to change. He was happy with his life. He slept till noon most days, hung out either watching television or listening to music until it was time to go out with his friends.

He'd had jobs before, but his mother had always been all right when he'd quit them and offered to help her. The only thing that had changed that he could see was Hank. Who was this guy anyway?

The good news was that Hank wouldn't be around long, Bo told himself. Not once he got to know Arlene. But Bo feared he couldn't wait that long. He was going to have to take matters into his own hands.

Either he had to find Charlotte and get her butt back here, or he was going to have to sabotage this little romance between his mother and Hank Monroe.

He called his friend Cody, since his car was in the shop and his mother had refused to let him drive hers. "Pick me up tonight. My mom has a date and there's something we need to do. Bring a crowbar. And if you have a ski mask, bring that, too."

ARLENE WAS GETTING ready for her date with Hank when the phone rang. She hurriedly reached for it, praying it was Charlotte.

The voice on the other end of the line was authoritative, and she knew from experience whoever was calling was going to give her bad news.

"Is it Charlotte?" she cried, just wanting to get the worst over with.

"I beg your pardon? This is Dr. Ray Hamilton calling from the state hospital in regard to your daughter Violet."

Violet? Had she been released? Was she on her way

here? Arlene glanced toward the dark windows and thought Bo was right. She didn't want to be here alone.

"Is she…?" Arlene couldn't form the words.

"We are required by law to let you know that Violet will be leaving our facility in a few weeks."

"Leaving for where?"

"She is being released on her own since she is an adult, Mrs. Evans. I'm sure you were told about your daughter's medical breakthrough."

"No. You're wrong. You don't know Violet. If you let her out—"

"I'm sorry you feel that way, but I'm afraid the evaluation of her mental health isn't up to you. We are just required to let you know. Good day, Mrs. Evans."

"No," Arlene said into the phone even though she knew the doctor had hung up.

Violet was getting out.

She stood in her bedroom too stunned to move. Hadn't she known that her life had been going too well? The business? And Hank?

Hank. She felt her heart sink. For just a few hours she'd let herself believe she could be happy.

Not that she'd ever thought she deserved it.

She reached for the phone and dialed Hank's number, telling herself it was for the best. Better to end it before it was started. Better to end it before he did.

She glanced toward the chair where her mother had sat for years.

You're right, Mother. It's all my fault. You told me I would end up alone. You were right. That must make you very happy.

She made a swipe at her tears. Hank's line was busy. She'd have to try again in a few minutes.

Facing the mirror, she straightened her shoulders and lifted her chin. She would face this alone. It wasn't as if she hadn't been here before.

"WHO IS THIS GUY anyway?" Cody asked as he and Bo drove into Hank Monroe's ranch.

"We're about to find out." Bo had waited until he'd seen Hank drive out before he'd instructed Cody to drive down the hill to the huge ranch house. No one should live in such a large house. Especially some dude living by himself, Bo thought angrily.

"You sure he doesn't have someone working for him?" Cody asked, sounding nervous.

"I asked around," Bo said. "Hank has a bunch of land, but the only animals on the place are a couple of horses. He has Claudia Nicholson come out twice a week and clean. There's no security system."

Cody pulled up in front of the house, cut the engine and sat for a moment, staring at the house. "Is the guy crazy?"

"Apparently so, since he's dating my mother," Bo quipped. "Come on." He opened his door and climbed out.

"What exactly are we looking for?" Cody asked.

"Whatever we can find." Something incriminating. So he could tell his mother what he suspected she already suspected: Hank Monroe *was* too good to be true. Bo was counting on it as he picked up a rock to bust a window.

"This guy *is* a fool," Cody said as he tried the front door and it swung open. "The door wasn't even locked." His friend made a face as Bo dropped the rock. "I don't like this. Seems a little too easy, you know?"

Bo knew. "The guy is clueless. Don't worry about it." He shoved past Cody and entered the cool, dim, massive living room. Hank Monroe apparently had money. But how had he made it?

"Where do we start?" Cody asked as they took in the place. "Nice. Maybe it wouldn't be so bad if he married your mother."

"He's not going to marry her," Bo snapped. "No one marries someone like her unless he has to." He'd heard how she'd come to marry Floyd Evans; he'd overheard his grandmother Evans talking about it. Floyd Evans wouldn't have married her except that she'd been pregnant with Violet.

"Still, what does it hurt having a guy like this dating your mother?"

Bo ignored the question. He didn't like talking about his mother's love life. He couldn't imagine what Hank saw in her. The guy had to be up to something.

Cody followed him down the hallway.

"You check the bedroom," Bo ordered. "Look for drugs or anything weird." He stepped into what was obviously a home office and went straight to the file cabinet first. He had no idea what he was looking for, but he didn't find anything interesting and turned to the computer.

The computer appeared to be brand-new, state-of-the-art, and it didn't have anything on it except the software it had come with.

Discouraged, he glanced around the room, his gaze falling on the answering machine—and the flashing red light.

He reached over and hit the play button.

HANK FELT HIS CELL phone vibrate when he was not two miles from the ranch. While he didn't lock the doors at the ranch, he did have a security system of sorts: when a door was opened, he got a call on his cell. And since this wasn't the day that Claudia Nicholson cleaned, he turned around and sped back toward the ranch.

He took the back way in and, as he came over a hill, met with a road full of cattle and two cowboys on horses herding the slow-moving cows to another pasture.

That cost him valuable time.

He parked just over the hill from the house and took out the gun he kept taped on the underside of the SUV seat.

Crickets chirped in the tall green grass as he made his way toward the house. The evening breeze stirred the stand of ponderosas, sending the scent of pine wafting through the warm air. In the distance, the Little Rockies range slowly turned from violet to black against the midnight-blue sky.

Hank could feel the air grow heavy around him, the heft of the gun too familiar in his hand. He'd been here before, too many times, and had thought he'd put this part of his life behind him.

Right. That's why you keep guns stashed in places easy to get to should you need them.

The back door was unlocked. He turned the knob without making a sound and stepped in. The air inside felt cool and smelled of the orange-scented cleaner Claudia used.

The back door opened into the laundry room. He stepped from it to the doorway to the kitchen. Empty.

He moved quickly through the large commercial kitchen, into the open living area with its huge fireplace and assorted leather furniture. The ranch house had come furnished. He had yet to sit in every chair.

Shoving away the thought of how ridiculous that was, he glanced down the hallway, pretty sure whoever had been here was gone.

But he gripped the gun as he moved down the hallway, not willing to take the chance he was wrong. He wasn't a man who took chances. That's how he'd managed to live this long.

At his office, he looked in and saw that his chair had been moved and one of the file cabinets wasn't closed all the way.

As he moved down the hallway, he noted that there were tracks in the thick, recently vacuumed carpet. He checked each room, which took him some time. Another problem with having a house this size.

Finding nothing, he returned to the office. What had the intruder been looking for?

Nothing appeared to be missing. Not his expensive stereo equipment, wide-screen televisions or artwork. But then, his intruders—from the tracks in the thick carpet, there had been two of them—hadn't had enough time to do much damage.

All of it could have been replaced. None of it had any sentimental value. He liked it that way. He'd already lost the important things in his life.

He checked the file cabinet first. Nothing missing. He didn't bother with the computer, since there was nothing on it to steal.

Sitting down at his desk, he considered who might have been here. He glanced at the answering machine. No messages.

The phone rang, startling him. He let the machine pick up.

"Hank?" Arlene's voice, worry in her tone. "I'm not going to be able to make our date tonight. I'm sorry. I... Something's come up."

He started to reach for the phone, but she hung up too quickly. He was worrying that she'd heard something about Charlotte. He hit rewind to play her message again to gauge how much worry he'd heard.

The machine seemed to rewind a little too long, and then he realized why. There'd been another new message.

"Hank. It's Cameron. Call me. Something has come up of grave importance. It concerns you, I'm afraid, and could be dire."

There was a pause, then Arlene's message. The answering machine shut off, throwing the room into a dense silence that was almost palpable.

Hank swore. Cam wasn't leaving his messages in code any longer. What the hell had happened that Cam would be calling? Grave importance? Something concerning him that could be dire?

Hank swore again. They weren't going to draw him back in. He didn't care what the problem was. He was done with that life.

As he reached over to erase the tape, he realized that whoever had been in the house had played the message. That's why the light hadn't been flashing. His intruders had listened to Cam's message.

"THAT WAS TOO CLOSE, man," Cody said as they sped down the road. "If you hadn't looked out the back way and seen him coming... He had a *gun*."

"Yeah, what was that about?" Bo was still panting. They'd pushed Cody's car out of the drive so Hank couldn't hear them start up the engine and come hauling ass after them. "What's the guy doing with a gun?"

Cody shot him a look. "Who cares? He's dangerous. And if he finds out we were in his house—"

"He won't," Bo snapped, not sure of that at all. How had the dude known in the first place? And who was this guy anyway? he thought, remembering what he'd heard on the answering machine. And what kind of crap was Hank Monroe involved in?

Unfortunately Bo hadn't a clue. The house was expensive as all hell and impersonal, as if Hank Monroe wasn't staying long. He was hiding something, that was a given. The question was how to find out what.

"Let's stop by your place. I need to use your computer," Bo said.

"Tell me why I had to bring along a crowbar and a ski mask so you could call up a porn site on my computer?" Cody said belligerently. "I thought we were going to do something fun?"

"I'm not after porn," Bo snapped. "I'm trying to find out more about Hank Monroe. Look," he said, "after I'm done, we'll go buy some beer and see if we can find those girls we saw the other night. What do you say?"

HANK CALLED ARLENE from his cell. "Sorry, I'm running a little late. They're moving cattle out by me."

"You didn't get my message?" she asked. "No, I guess you'd already left."

"Did you hear from Charlotte?" he asked, hoping that's

all it had been: Charlotte had come home and Arlene needed to stay with her daughter tonight.

"No, nothing."

"Are you all right?" he asked.

"Sure. That is, I'll be fine."

He didn't doubt that. She was strong. She wouldn't have gotten this far if she wasn't. From the moment he'd met her he'd known her life had been hell. Maybe that was why he'd asked her out.

He'd seen himself in her.

"You can tell me what's happened when I pick you up," he said. "Get dressed. I made reservations for the play at the theater in Fort Peck. I haven't been there yet, but I hear the building is something to see and the performances are wonderful."

"I don't think that's a good idea." Arlene hesitated. "I got a call about my oldest daughter. I haven't told you about Violet."

"You can tell me about her on the way."

"And ruin a perfectly good date?" Arlene said with a humorless laugh.

"Nothing could ruin our date. Trust me, you'd be surprised what it takes to shock me. Get dressed, wear something casual. I'm on my way."

ARLENE HUNG UP THE phone, so touched by Hank's understanding and kindness that her eyes were swimming again in tears. She made an irritated swipe at them. She acted as if no one had ever been kind to her.

You don't deserve this.

Her mother again. So maybe it was true that she hadn't

gotten a lot of compassion. The thought made her laugh. Her mother and compassion had never crossed paths.

But how *had* Arlene gotten so lucky to have Hank Monroe in her life? Even for a while?

He wants something from you. He'll hurt you just like all men.

Arlene turned on the radio to drown out her mother's voice and dressed quickly, not wanting to be late. As she dabbed on a little lip gloss, she caught her reflection in the mirror. For a moment she was taken aback. She didn't recognize the woman looking back at her.

There was color in her cheeks, and her eyes seemed to twinkle. She smiled at her reflection, almost embarrassed by what she saw—because she hadn't seen it in so long she had trouble even putting a name to it. Joy.

Instantly she turned from the mirror. How could she go on a date as if Charlotte wasn't missing and eight months pregnant? As if Violet wasn't getting out of the mental hospital and homicidal? As if Bo wasn't somewhere getting in trouble instead of looking for a job?

The phone rang, and for an instant her heart sank. It would be Hank canceling. He would have had time to rethink their date. He would make some lame excuse.

She braced herself for the worst. It wasn't as if she hadn't been here before. "Hello?"

"It's me."

"Charlotte? Oh, my God, you have had me worried out of my mind. Where are you? Are you all right?"

"I'm fine. I just called to tell you that the father of my baby and I are going away to make a life for ourselves. Don't come looking for me. I'll write as soon as we get settled."

"The *baby?*" Arlene cried.

"It hasn't come yet. I had some false labor, but I'm fine. I'll call you when the baby comes."

"Charlotte, wait. I…" But the line had gone dead.

Arlene stood for a moment holding the phone. All her worry, and Charlotte was fine. She felt anger well inside her at her youngest daughter for scaring her so and waited for the relief to sink in as she hung up the phone.

Her children were no longer children. She'd protected them for years when she should have made them take responsibility for their own actions. But she'd wanted so badly to be a good mother. A perfect mother. And she'd gotten it all wrong.

She'd become her mother.

There was a horrible thought.

She replayed Charlotte's words in her head, still waiting for the relief to wash over her. Charlotte was fine. And yet Arlene had no idea where she was or who she was with or when she would hear from her again. Nor would she get to see her first grandbaby born.

She straightened and met her gaze in the mirror again, determination burning in her eyes.

She didn't deserve a second chance, not with the mess she'd made of her life. But if Hank was giving her one, damned if she wasn't going to take it.

"THANK YOU FOR TONIGHT," Arlene said when he parked in front of her house later that evening. "I had a wonderful time."

"My pleasure. I'm glad you heard from Charlotte. I

still might try to find out who she left town with, if you don't mind."

"No, I appreciate it. But are you sure you want to do that?"

He laughed. "I've always been a big fan of mysteries. I can't stand it when I can't figure out the ending. I never cheat, though," he said quickly, making her smile. "But I am also seldom wrong about who did it."

"You would have made a good cop," she said. "You would have been the one who never gave up until he caught the bad guys."

She didn't know how close she'd come to the truth. Or maybe she did. Arlene was a lot sharper than he guessed people had ever given her credit for.

"That would have been me, all right." He'd always loved the chase. It had gotten into his blood—and cost him dearly. Cost him his family. And for a while he'd been afraid it would cost him his soul. He still wasn't sure it hadn't.

Leaning toward her, he kissed her gently on the lips. It felt so good he drew her to him. She felt stiff in his arms at first. He took his time, kissing her slowly, gently, teasing her lips and the tip of her tongue with his own.

He felt her shock the first time his tongue ran over the tip of her own. A soft chuckle emanated from him. A pleased chuckle as he drew her even closer.

He could feel her pulse pounding as he cupped her jaw, his thumb caressing her skin. She sighed against his lips.

Pulling back to look into her eyes, he could see that her cheeks were flushed with pleasure, her eyes bright. He smiled at her, wanting to brush his fingers along her collarbone to unhook the top button of her shirt and reveal the swell of her full breasts.

He wanted to make love to her, slowly and tenderly. To arouse what he sensed in her was a passion that she kept tightly reined in.

"I should get in the house," she said, sounding out of breath.

He nodded as he started to get out to walk her to the door.

"No, please," she said, opening her door and quickly slipping out. She bent to look in at him. "Thank you again. Good night."

"Good night." He sighed as she hurriedly closed the door and strode up the steps to disappear inside the dark house. Apparently Bo wasn't home.

Hank hesitated a moment, not liking the idea of her being out here all alone. Then he reminded himself that Arlene was probably as capable as anyone of surviving in this part of the country. It wasn't as if her children had ever been there for her.

He recalled what she'd told him about Violet, her oldest.

"I didn't know what to do," Arlene had said in tears. "I wanted to get her help when I'd seen that something was wrong with her when she was just a girl. But my mother, my mother-in-law and Floyd forbade it. I should have done it anyway. I should—"

Hank had touched her lips with a finger. "You have to stop blaming yourself. She's getting the help she needs now at the state mental hospital, right?"

Arlene had looked over at him and he'd seen the fear

in her eyes. "She has everyone fooled. They're going to let her out, and I'm just terrified of what she'll do."

As he drove away now, he feared Arlene had reason to be afraid.

Chapter Five

The next morning Hank asked himself what he was doing as he parked in front of the Cut and Curl beauty shop where Charlotte Evans had worked.

Charlotte had called her mother and said she was with the father of her baby and making a new life somewhere else. So why didn't he just let it go?

Because of Arlene. She should have been relieved, but he'd known that something had been bothering her last night and, finally, on the way home he'd asked her what it was.

"Don't you realize just the thought of Violet getting out of the mental hospital is enough to have me worried?" she'd asked. "She hates me, blames me for everything. Not that I'm *not* to blame."

"You didn't make Violet into an attempted murderer," he'd assured her. "A lot of kids grow up in horrible environments where they don't get enough food and are beaten every day and they don't become killers. You aren't responsible for what Violet did."

"She tried to kill me. Her own mother." Arlene's voice had broken. "She even got her brother and sister involved."

He'd reached over and taken her hand. "They failed. That should tell you something."

Arlene had laughed and made a swipe at her tears. "That my children fail at everything? No," she'd said, sobering, "*I* failed *them*."

He'd chuckled at that. "Don't you think a lot of parents feel that way? My daughter won't even talk to me. She hates me—and rightfully so. I wasn't there for her. I was busy with my job, but I told myself that she was better off being raised by her mother than me."

"I'm sorry."

"It's my own fault. We all make choices. At the time we think they're the best ones. It isn't until later, hindsight being twenty-twenty, that we wish we'd done it differently."

Arlene had nodded. "There are no second chances."

"I'm not so sure about that." He'd glanced over at her, her face silhouetted against the night prairie. The Larb Hills had been a deep purple as they paralleled Highway 2. The sky overhead had been a dense dark canopy except for the twinkling lights of a zillion stars. Hank had never seen so many stars.

"It isn't just Violet," Arlene had said after a few moments. "It's Charlotte. She sounded so…matter-of-fact on the phone. So distant."

That, Hank realized now, was what had his instincts telling him that something was wrong. If the girl really had run off with the father of her baby, wouldn't she be triumphant? Especially if the man was married. It would mean she'd won him. And she'd be gloating, knowing all of this would hurt her mother. Relieving her mother's mind was the last thing Charlotte Evans would do, from what he could gather.

He hesitated before getting out of the SUV. What he was about to do was more than illegal, impersonating an FBI agent.

And, possibly worse, he would call attention to himself. Enough people in town wondered who he was, what he did for a living and why he'd picked Whitehorse, Montana. He didn't need any more rumors circulating.

Once he went into the beauty shop and impersonated an FBI agent, word would get out. Word might even get back to the agency where he'd really worked, and that was the last thing he needed, since Cameron was already trying to get in touch with him. He hadn't returned the calls, telling himself Cam would do anything to draw him back in.

But wasn't what he was doing right now just as bad?

He could just imagine what Bitsy would have to say. *You just can't help yourself, can you?*

He thought of the times he'd promised her he was going to get out of the business, spend more time at home.

While he doubted Bitsy had really believed it, he told himself he'd meant it at the time. Maybe he'd been lying to himself about that—just as he had everything else.

He'd been good at what he did. So was it any surprise a part of him missed it? Maybe just a little?

The bell over the door jangled as he stepped inside. All heads turned. A middle-aged stylist was giving an elderly woman a perm. A twentysomething was bent over another twentysomething's hand, giving her a manicure. All except the elderly woman getting her hair done wore pale pink shop smocks indicating they worked there, including the teenager sitting behind a small desk, doodling on a scratch pad. Business was obviously slow.

He saw at once that everyone except the elderly woman knew who he was. Having always lived in a big city, this small-town lack of anonymity continued to amaze him. How could there ever be any secrets?

"Hello," he said as he entered the room. The smell of perm solution was strong, but not as strong as the nail products.

"If you're looking for a haircut—" the middle-aged woman began.

"Just information," he said, garnering everyone's attention again as he pulled what could have been law-enforcement credentials from his wallet. What he flashed them, was, in fact a medical insurance card.

He'd discovered a long time ago that attitude was the key. "I'm trying to find Charlotte Evans."

"What's she done?" the teenager asked, no longer doodling.

"Can you tell me the last time you saw her?" he asked, ignoring the teen and directing his questions to the older of the bunch. "I'm sorry, I didn't catch your name."

"Tamara Lawson. I own the place. But Charlotte doesn't work here anymore. She hasn't for months."

"But she worked here when she became pregnant," he said.

"That wasn't our fault," the teen said with a giggle.

Tamara shot her a look. He saw the resemblance between the two and guessed the teen must be her daughter.

"What's going on?" the elderly woman demanded loudly. He saw that her hearing aid was sitting on the counter.

"It's nothing to concern yourself with, Mabel," Tamara shouted back at the woman.

The dark-haired twentysomething getting her nails done laughed at what the teen had said.

Hank smiled. "But you knew about the pregnancy. And you are…?"

"Jana. Charlotte was barfing all the time. How could we not know about it?"

"She tell you who the father was?" Hank asked.

They all shared a look, and the manicurist went back to work on Jana's nails.

"She tell you something, miss?" he asked the young woman doing her coworker's nails.

"Linsey," she said.

"Charlotte got knocked up on purpose," the teen said, obviously hating being ignored. "At least that's what she told us."

"Sahara," her mother chastised.

"I wouldn't be asking if it wasn't important," Hank said. "Charlotte seems to have disappeared."

Jana made a disbelieving sound.

"Anything you tell me will be held in the strictest of confidence," he added.

"What does he want?" the elderly woman shouted.

"A haircut," Tamara shouted back as she finished Mabel's last curl and stuck her under the dryer.

"Do you know Charlotte?" Tamara asked him as she walked away from the client and the noisy dryer.

He shook his head. "She could be in trouble."

"She's always in trouble," Tamara said with a shake of her head.

It felt like old times. He waited a beat, then said quietly, "Tell me about the father of the baby."

"All we know is what she told us. It was some man she met one night at the café. She worked here and at the Northern Lights restaurant for a while. I got the impression he was a lot older and married."

"She said she put something in his drink," the teen interjected.

"She drugged him?" Hank asked, no surprise in his voice.

"She wanted a baby," the teen said.

"At least at that moment," Tamara said, seeming to have given up on shutting up the teen.

"Does the father know about the baby?" he asked.

Tamara shook her head. "I'm not even sure she knew his name."

"Do you know where he was staying?"

Silence. Then Sahara said, "She took him to the Shady Rest Motel." The teen looked indignant. "I know because Charlotte said he was so out of it she charged the room to his credit card."

Hank nodded. A credit card. Perfect. "And you say he was married?" he asked Linsey.

Clearly she didn't want to be the one to tell him anything. Had she and Charlotte been friends?

"He told Charlotte he was separated and getting a divorce, but I think that was just a line," Linsey finally confided.

Smart girl.

"She doesn't want the baby, you know," the teen said. "But she won't give it up for adoption because her mother wants her to."

Everyone shot the girl a look.

"Well, it's true," the teen said.

ARLENE HAD NEVER missed entering her baked goods in a county fair since the age of eleven. She loved to bake and prided herself on her pie crusts, her moist yet light-as-air cakes and her cookies, especially her gingersnaps.

For years she'd used baking as a way to relax. It was something she could do well—one of the few things.

That's why it surprised her the morning after her date with Hank that she didn't feel like baking.

"So how was your date?" Bo asked as he came into the kitchen.

"Fine. How is your job hunt going?" she asked.

"I thought you'd be baking by now. Where's your rejects?"

Her "rejects" were cookies that weren't quite perfect. She'd never realized before that Bo paid any attention to fair time. Apparently he did. For a while she'd had all her blue ribbons displayed in the living room. Since she met Hank, she'd moved them into her sewing room. Funny how she didn't feel the need to validate herself with blue ribbons with him.

"I don't think I'm going to enter after all this year," she said. "With Charlotte gone and—"

"I don't believe this," Bo snapped. "You're changing your whole life over a man."

"That's not true. Maybe it's just that I have enough blue ribbons. I don't need any more. I *know* I'm a good cook."

He stared at her. "You're going to let one of the Cavanaughs take your blue ribbons?"

Bo knew exactly what to say to get her worked up. She'd always been envious of the Cavanaughs. Pearl and her husband Titus were like royalty in Old Town Whitehorse. And their granddaughters, Laci and Laney, were princesses. Same with the Baileys. Eve, Faith and Mc-Kenna Bailey were beauties.

Since Arlene married Floyd Evans, she'd felt she'd needed to prove something to the elite families of Old Town.

Bo's words brought back that familiar insecurity. Maybe she *should* enter. She didn't want the whole county speculating on why she hadn't.

But as quickly as the feeling came, it passed. Was she tired of trying to prove herself to people who had never accepted her anyway?

"Laci Cavanaugh is a great cook," she said. "I'll be interested to see what she enters. I'm sure she'll do well."

"You're starting to scare me," Bo mumbled as he left the room.

Arlene didn't even hear the blare of his stereo down the hall. She was thinking about last night at the play. And Hank.

HANK COULDN'T HELP worrying as he left the beauty shop. It had almost been too easy. Charlotte was young, indiscreet and, he suspected, liked to shock people. Her blatant disregard for social mores had apparently disavowed any loyalty her coworkers might have had for her.

Except Linsey, who had made an effort not to talk about Charlotte. She had one friend, anyway.

The ease of getting the information wasn't what bothered him. It was Charlotte sharing it with everyone. Being a suspicious person, Hank felt as if the girl had tried to sell her story a little too hard.

Had she just been trying to cover up the identity of the

man who had really fathered her baby? A local man she'd now run off with?

Whoever he was, the man didn't live in Whitehorse or Hank suspected it would be all over town that he'd left. Unless no one knew yet that he'd left with Charlotte.

Still, Hank couldn't shed the feeling that something wasn't right. Charlotte wasn't the kind of young woman who felt the need to come up with an elaborate plan just so she could run away.

The car stashed in the ravine worried him. Why hide the car? She had no reason to think anyone would come after her, so she didn't need to buy time. She could have left the car parked in town somewhere. Or even left it beside the road. Why go to the trouble, eight months pregnant, of ditching her car that way?

The engine grease on the steering wheel also bothered him. He wondered if he could get a clear print. It was worth a try. He'd love to narrow down who'd been with Charlotte that day on the road.

But it meant calling on a few old friends. It wasn't like they didn't know where he was, he thought, reminded of Cam's calls. So why not see if he could track down this mystery man of Charlotte's?

By late afternoon, Hank had the name of the man Charlotte Evans had checked into the Shady Rest Motel with eight months before. But, Hank reminded himself, this might not even be the father of Charlotte's baby. There was more than a good chance the girl had lied to the women she'd worked with, for whatever reason.

He called Arlene. "I have a possible lead. According

to her coworkers, Charlotte told them the man was from out of town."

"Her coworkers told you that? They wouldn't give me the time of day."

"I was very persuasive and they don't know me," he said. It also helped that he'd let them believe he was a lawman of some sort.

"The man lives in Billings, was just in town for a couple of nights and apparently met Charlotte at the restaurant where she was working," Hank said. "It seems Charlotte was determined to get pregnant and may have picked him because he was from out of town."

"Oh, my God," Arlene said. "Do you think Charlotte is with him?"

"Maybe, although I doubt it. He told her he was separated from his wife and getting a divorce, but more than likely he lied about that. But he could have heard from her." Hank wondered, though, what the man would have done if Charlotte had gone to him for help. Especially if he had later realized that she'd drugged him and set him up. Most men wouldn't have taken that well.

"The man's name is John Foster," Hank said. "I thought we might take a road trip and have a little talk with him."

THE FOSTERS LIVED in a house on the rims—a unique geological feature of Montana's largest city, Billings.

The house was large and expensive, the landscaping extensive with a picturesque view of the Yellowstone River valley.

Hank rang the bell and glanced over at Arlene. "You all right?"

She nodded.

"Keep in mind, he might not be the father of Charlotte's baby."

"I know."

"Would you rather wait in the car?"

She smiled. "Are you worried I'm going to make a scene?"

"I wouldn't blame you."

"No," she said and touched his cheek. "You wouldn't."

The door opened. A Hispanic woman of indeterminate age asked in broken English, "May I help you?"

"We're here to see Mr. Foster. John Foster," Hank said.

Before the woman could answer, a tall, thin, thirty-something man appeared behind her. "I'll take care of this, Delores."

Delores quickly disappeared down a hallway.

John Foster frowned as he came forward. "What is this about?"

"We need to speak to you about a missing person," Hank said.

"Are you…police?" he asked, shifting his gaze to Arlene.

"Do you mind if we step inside, Mr. Foster? I'm sure we can clear this up quickly if you'll just answer a few questions about your stay in Whitehorse, Montana."

John Foster's already pale face blanched bone-white. He looked as if he might pass out.

"I don't know what you're talking about," he said.

"Maybe your wife can help us," Hank suggested.

"She isn't here." His voice broke. "Please. My wife doesn't know. She's shopping, but she could come home at any moment."

"Then I suggest you answer our questions before she gets back," Hank said, surprised Arlene was letting him handle this. He knew that wasn't her nature. She'd had to handle everything for years without any help. Maybe that's why she was being so quiet now.

"Come in, then," John Foster said and quickly led them down the hallway to what appeared to the den and home office. He closed the door behind them, but didn't offer them a chair.

Hank produced the photograph Arlene had given him of Charlotte and watched the man's expression. He knew now where the phrase *guilty as sin* came from.

"When was the last time you saw her?" Hank asked.

"I only saw her that one time. In Whitehorse. I swear." His eyes were wide with fear. "She told me she was twenty-one."

"And you believed her?" Arlene asked sarcastically.

"Oh, God, don't tell me she's—"

"No, she's not a minor," Hank said. "She's eighteen. And pregnant."

They had been standing in a large den furnished in lush carpet and deep leather chairs around a massive cherrywood desk.

John Foster dropped into one of the chairs like a puppet whose strings had just been severed. "*Pregnant?* No."

"You didn't think to use protection?" Arlene asked.

"Look, I don't even remember what happened. I swear to you I didn't think I had that much to drink. I woke up the next morning and she was gone. I thought I'd dreamed it."

"Sure you did," Arlene said.

"The girl hasn't contacted you since?" Hank asked, although from John Foster's reaction, Hank would have sworn the man hadn't known about the pregnancy. If Charlotte had contacted him, it would probably have been for money. The baby would have been the leverage.

"I swear I never saw or heard from her again. You have to believe me. Please, my wife hasn't been well. I don't want her—"

Following a soft tap, the office door swung open and a women in her early thirties peered in. "Oh, I'm sorry. I heard voices. I didn't realize we had company."

Between her dress and her composure, Hank guessed she was Mrs. Foster. What took him by surprise was the fact that the woman was very pregnant.

John was on his feet and practically wringing his hands. "Meredith, this is—"

"We're here as part of an investigation involving a missing young woman from Whitehorse, Montana," Hank said, interrupting him. Her hand was cool to the touch as cool as the lady herself.

Meredith Foster lifted one perfect eyebrow. *"Whitehorse?"*

"Your husband spent a couple of nights in Whitehorse about eight months ago," Hank said. Out of the corner of his eye he saw that John Foster looked about to hyperventilate.

"I don't understand," Meredith said.

"The young woman in question waited on your husband at a restaurant called Northern Lights," Hank said.

Meredith Foster laughed. "You're questioning everyone who this woman waited on eight months ago?"

"Just those individuals who might have felt sorry for her and offered to help her," Hank said.

Meredith finally looked at her husband. "My husband is a kind man. If the woman was in some sort of trouble…"

"Your husband was seen consoling her after she dropped one of the patron's meals," Hank said.

"Well, that explains it, doesn't it?" she said. "I'm willing to bet he also left her a large tip. John is very generous."

"Yes, he did leave a *very* large tip," Hank said.

Meredith's laugh reminded him of wind chimes as she stepped to her husband. She wrapped long, manicured fingers around his forearm as if to hug him. Or steady him.

"I'm sorry this young woman ran away," she said as she placed her other hand on her protruding belly. "Her mother must be worried sick." Her gaze flicked to Arlene.

Hank took a notepad from the desk and a pen. "This is my cell phone number. If you think of anything else or happen to see or hear from her—"

"Why would she contact my husband?" Meredith asked, seeming to lose a little of her cool.

"He was kind to her. She could have gotten his name from his credit card. If she was in trouble, she might reach out to him," Hank said, then tipped his Western hat. "I'm sorry if I upset you. Your husband mentioned you hadn't been well…?"

"I've had a difficult pregnancy," she said, her hand again going to her stomach.

"When are you due?" Arlene asked.

"Next month," Meredith said and smiled up at her husband. "We can't wait for the baby to be born."

"You don't know if it's a girl or a boy?" Arlene asked.

"No," Meredith said, cutting her gaze to Arlene. "I want to be surprised."

"THEY'RE LYING," Arlene said the moment they were in Hank's SUV. "At least she is. She knows about her husband and Charlotte."

Hank looked over at Arlene as he started the engine, admiring her instincts, especially since they so closely coincided with his own. "She's covering for him, I agree. But I don't think he knew Charlotte was pregnant—or that his wife was onto him."

"So you think he's the father of Charlotte's baby?" Arlene asked. "He's obviously been quite busy."

"Hard to say until Charlotte's baby is born and a DNA test can be administered," Hank said. "But I'd say he's afraid he is. And so is his wife."

"That doesn't help us find Charlotte," Arlene said. "Maybe he isn't the father. Maybe Charlotte is with the father of her baby right now, safe somewhere."

Maybe. "Well, the one thing I think we can count on is that Charlotte isn't being kept locked in the basement of the Foster house."

"No," she agreed distractedly. "You didn't tell me about what happened at the restaurant."

He looked straight ahead as he pulled out into the street. He hadn't told her, either, that a woman matching Meredith Foster's description had been to the restaurant asking about Charlotte. "I should have told you, but you already had enough to worry about."

"Well, you're wrong. I can take it."

He smiled over at her. "I never doubted that. That's one of the things I admire about it. You're a survivor, Arlene."

ARLENE LAUGHED at that, shaking her head as she studied him. She'd quit asking herself why he was doing this. Clearly he was enjoying it. And he was very good at this intrigue business. Maybe too good at it?

"You never told me what kind of business you were in before you retired," she said, watching his reaction to her question.

He kept his gaze on the road. "Corporation stuff, not very interesting."

She said nothing, hearing the lie and feeling a little ill. She turned away to stare out her side window. Just when she was starting to trust him. Was even trusting him with Charlotte's and her grandbaby's lives.

Suddenly he pulled off the road, cut the engine and turned to her. "I worked for the government. I don't want to lie to you. But I also can't tell you exactly who I worked for or what I did. Let's just say it was in security."

"Thank you," she said, looking into his eyes. They were a deep, rich brown. "Don't worry. I won't say anything to anyone, if that's what you're worried about."

"My wife got sick of the secrecy," he said, chewing at his cheek as he looked thoughtful. "So did I. But that life is behind me now."

The way he said it, she wondered whether he was trying to convince her or himself.

"We all right?" he asked.

She nodded and smiled over at him. "What do we do now?"

"We hope we hear from Charlotte," he said. "If John Foster is the father, then she hasn't contacted him."

"What about Meredith Foster?"

"I doubt Charlotte would try to run a blackmail scam on her," Hank said. "Even in her condition, difficult pregnancy and all, Meredith Foster isn't the pushover her husband apparently was. Charlotte wouldn't get anywhere with that woman."

Arlene couldn't argue that. Still, she wondered what a woman like that would do if she found out about her husband's affair—and the subsequent pregnancy.

Chapter Six

"It's all a horrible mistake," John Foster said the moment the two had left.

"Of course it is," Meredith agreed. "Why don't you make us both a drink and I'll tell you about my day."

John didn't move. "You aren't upset with me?"

"John," she said, cupping his cheek, "we agreed not to ever discuss those days you were gone. It doesn't matter. I know that whatever problems that waitress has, they have nothing to do with us. Now—that drink?"

He nodded quickly. "I just don't want you upset. The baby..."

She placed a hand over her stomach. "The baby is fine. Now, please, make yourself a martini. I'll take a mineral water with a wedge of lime."

He scurried away to the bar. Meredith Foster watched him go, wishing she didn't know her husband so well.

She had sensed something was wrong the moment John came in the front door eight months ago, suitcase in hand, hangdog look on his face after being gone for three days.

At the time she'd thought, *He's damned lucky I haven't had the locks changed yet.*

"Back to get the rest of your things?" she'd asked as disinterestedly as she could sound.

"I made a mistake," John had said, looking like a whipped puppy. "I haven't been myself lately. I don't really want a divorce. I don't even know why I said I did. I want to make our marriage work."

Meredith had been more startled and upset by this than when he'd asked for the divorce, packed a small suitcase and left, saying he'd be back for the rest of his things.

What had happened in the three days he'd been gone? Suddenly she'd been scared.

"I don't understand," she'd managed to say.

"I belong here with you," he'd said, sounding as if the words were very difficult for him.

She'd thought her father must have gotten to him. Or her father-in-law. The two older men were best friends, successful business partners and John's bosses.

"If that's what you're sure you want," she'd said graciously. "We won't ever speak of this again."

"Thank you, Meredith," he'd said quickly and given her an awkward hug and an even more awkward kiss. "I'll go up and unpack."

"No," she'd said. "Let me do that for you, John. Why don't you make us both a drink?"

He'd glanced at his suitcase, and she'd seen that he would have preferred to unpack it himself. Why was that?

She'd reached for the small suitcase. "I'll take a martini. You make such wonderful martinis."

He'd nodded and handed her the suitcase with obvious reluctance.

Upstairs, she'd placed the suitcase on the bed, taken a bracing breath, opened it. He hadn't taken much with him. Two casual shirts, jeans and some underwear.

She'd lifted out the wrinkled, obviously worn shirt on top. She'd been able to smell his scent on it—and another scent that had made her gag. Cheap perfume.

Repulsed, she'd leaned down to sniff the rest of the clothing in the suitcase. The cloying perfume had permeated everything, even those items he hadn't worn. The woman must have been all over him.

Meredith had dropped the shirt back into the suitcase and tried to get control of herself. It wasn't jealousy. She'd never loved John enough for that.

But she refused to let him jeopardize their lifestyle. She was content with John. She'd known what she was getting when she'd married him. She'd always believed that her father and father-in-law would keep John in line. What she hadn't seen coming was some midlife crisis at thirty-five.

She'd taken a couple of deep breaths as she'd heard John call up the stairs to her. Hurriedly she'd closed the suitcase and shoved it into the back of the closet.

She'd told herself she would deal with it later. Right then she'd needed to just make all of it go away. Her mother had taught her that the best way to deal with this sort of thing was to pretend it had never happened.

She'd checked herself in the mirror, brushed a lock of her hair back from her face, straightened to her full height and gone downstairs to have a pleasant evening with her husband.

The next morning, after a restless, sleepless night, she'd called her father. "John is back."

"I'm glad to hear he came to his senses."

Had he? Is that what had happened?

"I assume he will be back to work today, then?"

"He's on his way now. I'd prefer you not say anything to him."

Her father had grunted. "Fine, I guess. No reason to beat a dead horse."

She'd winced at his words. That morning John had seemed so cowed, so beaten down.

"Everything is back to normal, then?"

Normal. "Yes."

"I really wish you would reconsider having a baby," her mother had said when Meredith called her.

"You aren't suggesting that the only way I can hold on to my husband is to have a child, are you?"

Her mother hadn't been fazed. "A man is less likely to leave if there are children. Once men get restless, they need something to settle them down. John wouldn't dream of leaving you again if you were pregnant. And if the worst came to pass, a baby insures that a judge would make sure you can take the son of a bitch for everything. Without a baby, you might be forced to get a job."

She'd known her mother was right. The problem was that she didn't want a child, never had. Especially with John. "I like my life exactly as it is."

"Well," her mother had said, "I hope you get to keep it. But once they start asking for a divorce—"

"I have to go, Mother. I just wanted to tell you that John is back. Back to stay." She'd hung up more scared than angry, since she'd suspected her mother had already been down this rocky path. It would explain Meredith's four siblings, she feared.

When the credit card bills had come a month later, Meredith couldn't help but check the charges for the days when John had gone astray. Gas. She'd noted the Montana towns. Apparently he'd driven north out of Billings, buying gas at Roundup, Grass Range and Whitehorse. Twice in Whitehorse.

She'd glossed over the meal charges. Two charges on two separate nights at Northern Lights restaurant in Whitehorse. One almost double the cost of the first night. Apparently he hadn't eaten alone. Then she'd seen that he'd left a huge tip.

Alarms had begun to go off. She felt it had to be a mistake.

Her pulse had thundered as she'd checked the accommodation charges. Two nights in Whitehorse at the Milk River Lodge. Nothing odd about that, since he'd returned on the third night.

But…there'd been an additional room charge at the Shady Rest Motel for the same night he'd already paid for at the Milk River Lodge.

The evidence had been overwhelming.

The perfume on his clothing—she'd washed his clothing twice and aired out the suitcase, but she swore she could still smell that nauseating scent sometimes.

The room charges.

And John's guilt-ridden, shamed face when he'd returned home to her.

There'd been a woman.

A faceless, nameless woman in another town.

The man was an idiot. Didn't he realize he'd left a trail?

As she'd carefully refolded the credit card bill and put it in the bills-to-be-paid file, she'd known the best thing she could do was forget it. Men strayed.

Her own father had over the years. She remembered the way he'd return from a business trip with expensive presents for her mother—and herself. He'd always seemed a little cowed and contrite after one of those trips. Just as John had been.

Meredith had told herself that nothing could be gained by confronting her husband. The deed had been done. The best thing she could do was forget it had ever happened, just as she was sure John was trying to do.

But she'd been unable to shake the memory of that horrible perfume. Or the feeling that her marriage depended on knowing what had happened in Whitehorse.

"I'm going to go visit my friend Debra," she'd told John one morning at breakfast. Debra lived in Big Timber to the west. Nowhere near Whitehorse. "I'll be gone a few days."

"Don't worry about me," John had said distractedly. "I have a lot of work to do for your father."

"Delores will be here to make your meals."

"Fine." He'd been distracted since his return from Whitehorse. Polite. And preoccupied.

Meredith had known she had to find out if this other woman was a threat. She had to know for sure what had happened in Whitehorse—and with whom.

She'd packed a small bag. Her friend Debra had been in Europe for three weeks. Not that John would call to confirm where his wife had really gone. He would wait for Meredith to call him. She would use her cell phone and she would use cash. Unlike John, she was too smart to leave a trail.

Not that John would ever suspect her of anything. His mind didn't work that way. Or maybe he just didn't care enough to bother.

The thought had made her a little sad and she'd wondered why she was going to so much trouble. John wasn't worth fighting for. But her marriage and her position in the community *was,* she had reminded herself.

She was Mrs. John Foster and she was determined to remain so no matter what she had to do, she thought now as John handed her the glass of mineral water with a wedge of fresh lime and she took a drink, watching him over the rim of her glass, hating him more than he could imagine.

"I'VE BEEN THINKING," Hank said on the drive back to Whitehorse. "I'll do some checking on Mr. and Mrs. Foster and see what I can come up with."

Arlene let out a silent sigh of relief. "Thank you. There is something about that woman…"

"Yeah," he said and let out an oath as he came over a hill. "What the…?"

Below them was the Milk River valley, the trees along the river black compared to the lighter green hillsides. But it wasn't the valley or the few lights of town that could be seen that had caught his attention.

It was the northern horizon. Gigantic shafts of light shot up from it. Glowing white light, red, yellow, like a dozen colossal searchlights.

"It's the aurora borealis—the northern lights," Arlene

said, smiling at their effect on Hank. "I take it you've never seen them before?"

"I've heard of them, but I've never seen anything like this." There was awe in his voice, and he pulled over to the side of the road and got out. Arlene followed him as the luminous bands undulated, changing in color and brightness.

"They're believed to be electrical discharges in the ionized air," she said.

He smiled at that and put his arm around her as they watched. She loved that Hank Monroe could appreciate the simple things that Montana offered. He'd obviously seen the world, been places and seen and done things that other people couldn't even imagine. And yet he was standing here tonight with her, transfixed by something that to her was commonplace.

"I saw the lights once in the middle of the night when I was a girl," she said as they leaned back against the front of the SUV. "The sky was turquoise and bright as daylight."

"It's amazing," Hank said as he pulled her closer. She snuggled against him, and they stood like that watching the northern lights until the sky darkened again, the lights fading and finally disappearing.

"I'll never forget tonight," Hank said quietly as he turned her in his arms. His gaze locked with hers, and she knew even before he leaned toward her that he was going to kiss her.

The kiss rocked her. Not that she wasn't already on unstable ground just being in the man's arms. He cupped her face in his large hands, his touch gentle as he lowered his mouth to hers.

The kiss was soft and sweet as the summer night. A friendly kiss like a cool breeze. And then he pulled her closer, their bodies fitting together like puzzle pieces, and he turned up the heat. A scorching heat that warmed her to her toes and melted something inside her.

She let out a low moan as his fingers moved down the long column of her throat to stop on her throbbing pulse. And for just a moment his lips drew back. Their eyes met, a silent understanding passing between them, and then his mouth was on hers again, hot and demanding, and she was clutching at his shirt, balling the material in her fist as she opened to him.

Arlene knew what would have happened if the semi-truck hadn't come along when it did. She hardly noticed the glare of lights or the rumble of the engine as it came over the hill. But the blare of the horn definitely registered. She and Hank jumped apart as if stuck with a cattle prod.

The truck roared past, the driver giving the air horn another toot as he passed, his grinning face ghostly in the dim cab lights.

Hank laughed, the semi kicking up a small dust devil as it blew on by and down the hill into town.

Arlene watched the truck's taillights until it disappeared over a rise, too shaken to move. Darkness settled in around them, the northern lights long gone. She smoothed her shirt over her hips, feeling a little embarrassed—and disappointed.

Her heart was still pounding and as she touched her tongue to her lips, she could still feel him, still taste him on her.

"Well, that was one way to end a kiss," Hank said, sounding as taken aback as she felt. "I suppose I'd better get you home. It's later than I thought."

She nodded and walked around to climb back into his SUV. Neither said anything on the way to her house. He put a country-western station on the radio, and she settled into the seat. It felt so right being here with him. Just as the kiss had felt so right. And yet scary. She couldn't remember her heart ever pounding that hard. Certainly not when Floyd had made love to her. If that's what you called what he did to her.

"I'll call you tomorrow," Hank said as he walked her to the door. "Try not to worry about Charlotte. I'll continue doing what I can to find her."

"Thank you. Thank you for everything." She hurried inside, afraid what would happen if he kissed her again.

She stood just inside the door for a moment, listening to the quiet house. She could hear crickets outside the open windows, smell the freshly cut hay from the fields across the road, feel her own pulse thundering through her veins.

Hank had her heart pounding. She stood there, her whole body seeming to vibrate with the remembered feel of his mouth, his arms, the solid wall of his chest pressed against her breasts. Her nipples were still hard and painful beneath her bra. She'd felt Hank's kiss clear to her now-aching center.

As she moved down the hall without turning on a light, she was just thankful that neither Bo nor Charlotte was there right now. She knew even before she turned on the light in her bedroom, what she must look like.

It was an odd thing to stand before the large mirror and see herself with her face aglow, eyes bright and shiny as stars. She stood looking at the stranger in the mirror, enjoying this woman. How long had it been since she'd felt like a woman? Or had she ever?

Don't get too up on yourself.

That's mom talking, she warned herself.

She imagined her mother's pursed lips, the narrowed eyes and could almost see her sitting in that old rocker now reflected in the mirror.

Believe me, you have no reason to think you're anybody, little girl. Take a look in that mirror and tell me what you see. Nobody. So don't go getting on your high horse with me.

Arlene shook her head as she met her own eyes in the mirror and tried to shut out her mother's hurtful, horrible words.

"Just get home?" Bo asked behind her from the open doorway of her bedroom, making her jump.

She hadn't heard him come in and wondered why that was. Or had he been here all along? Waiting for her in the dark? Watching her and Hank? He'd wrecked his car some months back, and she'd told him he had to pay to have it repaired. Of course he hadn't. He'd just bummed rides off friends.

"How was your date?"

"Fine." No reason to correct him. Maybe it hadn't started out as a date, but it had surely ended as one, she thought, remembering Hank's arm around her as they'd watched the northern lights as if the show had been just for them. Not to mention the kiss.

"Is something wrong with you?" he asked. "You seem a little odder than usual."

His tone irritated her. "Did you want something?"

He shrugged. "I stopped by the mailbox on my way in." He handed her the stack of mail. Most of it, she knew, would be bills. "Just wanted to let you know I was home."

Home. The word grated on her. She knew Bo. He would push her to the max. "Bo?"

With obvious impatience, he turned back to her. *"What?"*

"How is the job hunting coming along?" she asked.

"Are you going to tell me to get a job every time you see me?" he snapped.

"If that's what it takes. I'll pick up some boxes in town tomorrow so you can start packing up your things."

He stared at her for a full minute, then shook his head. "You're making a mistake."

"The end of the week."

He shook his head again. "I guess this means I'm not your favorite anymore, huh." At one time she'd found it cute when he said things like that. She had played favorites with him. With Charlotte, too. It made her sick to admit it.

She thought of her brother. According to her mother, Carl could do no wrong. Unlike Arlene. The son was prized in the rural family. He was the male who would take over the place one day. He would build his bride a house on the property. His family would come over for dinner on Sundays. He was the one who stayed.

Daughters married and often moved away with their husbands. But sons in rural Montana stayed and worked the place with their fathers.

At least that was what Arlene had been raised to believe. Her brother had inherited the family farm in Chinook. And as awful as he'd treated their mother, he was still her favorite right up until the day she died.

After Floyd had left, Arlene had leased out this farm, since it had been clear Bo would never work it. If he got his hands on the place, he'd sell it and blow the money.

As she closed the door on her son and leaned against it, she understood that old expression, "This is hurting me more than it is you." She didn't want to lose her son. But the truth was, she'd lost all three of her children a long time ago.

She was through making excuses for them—and for herself. She couldn't change the past. But she could quit making the same mistakes.

As she thumbed through the mail—most of it just as she suspected: bills—she found the envelope addressed to her in Charlotte's feminine script and her heart leaped in her chest.

Hurriedly, she tore it open.

Mom, I'm fine. Sorry to leave the way I did. Don't worry about me or the baby. We'll be fine. Charlotte.

Arlene checked for a return address. None. The postmark was Whitehorse. Had Charlotte mailed this before she'd left? Or was she still in town?

Arlene reread it, finding a little peace in the words. It was so unlike Charlotte to write her a note of reassurance. But it was definitely Charlotte's handwriting.

She sat down on the bed, relief making her weak. Bo was banging around in his room, obviously angry.

"Hank put this into your head, didn't he?" Bo yelled from the other side of the door. "What do you know about this guy, anyway? Him and his big house, his nice car. You have any idea how he came by any of that? Or maybe what kind of past he has? He could be a criminal, for all you know."

She didn't answer as she carefully folded Charlotte's note, put it back in the envelope and placed it on the nightstand next to her bed. As she climbed into her bed, though, Bo's words echoed in her head.

What did she really know about Hank Monroe? He was kind, caring, generous, fun to be with, loving. And he'd reminded her what desire felt like. What more was there to know?

She thought about what he'd told her today in Billings. He'd worked for the government, some undercover-type agency.

What if he'd lied? Men do that all the time. Especially to get a woman in the sack.

To her surprise, it wasn't her mother's voice this time that she heard, but her own.

HANK DROVE TO THE ranch in a daze, his thoughts on Arlene and the night they'd just spent together watching the northern lights.

He was all the way across the porch, almost to his front door, when he realized he wasn't alone. He'd been so lost in his thoughts that he hadn't taken the usual precautions.

He turned quickly, coming face-to-face with his former boss. "Cameron?" Startled, Hank wondered if he had lost his edge. In the old days he would have known Cameron was there.

"You don't answer your messages."

"What the hell are you doing here?"

"You didn't return my phone calls. What was I supposed to do?"

"Leave me alone?"

Cameron shook his head. "I couldn't do that, Hank. I need your help."

Hank stepped back, still upset that he'd been so careless. He'd been thinking about Arlene. "I'm done with the agency."

"Come on, Hank. You can't run from this."

"Like hell I can't. I have enough money I can just keep right on going."

Cameron laughed and looked up at the stars. "As if you could find anywhere more remote than this. How the hell did you find this place?"

Hank didn't answer. He knew Cam was right. There was no place safe.

"I had no idea there were so many stars up there," Cameron said. "Or that you knew how to ride a horse," he said shifting his gaze to Hank. "I like the hat."

Hank swore under his breath.

"I could use a drink," Cameron said.

Knowing there was no way around this, Hank headed for the door. Best to get it over with and send Cameron on his way.

Hank went straight to the bar and poured them each a drink. He handed Cam one, knowing how his old friend and boss took his scotch. Neat. He motioned to one of the leather chairs and took his drink to a chair, as well.

"You're looking well," Hank said as he studied Cameron.

"Thanks. You're not looking so bad yourself. Not that you weren't always an ugly son of a bitch."

Hank smiled and took a slug of his drink. He was no beauty, that was for sure. His early years growing up in a rough mining town had left him with a repeatedly broken nose and more scars than he liked to count. If Cam hadn't taken him under his wing, Hank hated to think where he would have ended up. Probably in prison.

Instead Cameron Harris had taken all Hank's anger and aggression and turned him loose to play cops and robbers on a worldwide scale. While that meant Hank wouldn't see prison, it had certainly twisted his then already warped ideas of right and wrong.

"Now that we've covered the pleasantries, what the hell do you want?" Hank asked, knowing he was wrong for blaming Cameron for the way his life had turned out.

Cam didn't answer right away. He took a sip of his drink. "I didn't come here to screw up your new life."

Hank lifted a brow. "Oh, yeah?"

"I need you to look at some photographs."

Hank felt his belly tighten. *"Photographs?"*

Cameron nodded. "Twenty minutes, tops. Then I'm out of here and you won't be seeing me again."

"Me not seeing you doesn't means you won't be around," he said. "So let's see the photos." It was the last thing he wanted to do, but it was also the only way to get this over with.

Cam studied his drink for a moment, then finished it, set the glass on the table by his chair and rose. "I'll get them."

Hank finished his own drink and stood, too nervous to sit. He started to pour himself another drink, then thought better of it. He needed his wits about him.

Cam came back into the house a few minutes later with a black leather folder. He took it over to the breakfast bar. "You got a better light over here?"

Hank snapped on the overhead and Cam opened the folder.

The photographs were black-and-white, shot with a telephoto and a little grainy. Surveillance photos.

He studied the face at the center. The one in focus. And was relieved that he didn't recognize the man. He scanned the rest. All were of the same man.

"Don't know him," Hank said, pushing the photos away, relieved.

"Not the man," Cam said.

Hank shot him a look, that sick feeling back.

Cam reopened the folder to the first photograph. "The *woman*."

Hank looked down at the photograph again. He'd missed her the first time. She stood in the shadows, barely visible.

His heart began to pound. It *couldn't* be her.

Cam took a magnifying glass from his jacket pocket and slid it across the counter to him.

Hank didn't take it. Not until he'd flipped through all the photographs, stopping on one of the later shots.

His insides shaking, he picked up the magnifying glass and focused on the woman in the shadows—and felt his new world crumble around him.

A shaft of light from a street lamp had pierced the deep shadows and illuminated part of her face, more than enough to make a positive ID even if he hadn't been able to make out her trademark weapon she held at her side.

He followed her gaze across the photograph to the man at its center and knew even before he asked. "The man was the hit? He's dead?"

Cam nodded. "It's her, isn't it?"

Unable to look at the photograph any longer, Hank put down the magnifying glass and closed the folder.

It wasn't possible. And yet the photographs...

"When were these taken?"

"Last week in Prague," Cam said.

Hank walked over to the bar and poured himself a stiff drink, hating the fact that he needed it badly.

"You were the best," Cameron said, joining him. "Hell, you're a damned legend." He refilled his glass. "But, unfortunately, you're only as good as your last kill. People are asking questions."

"People?"

"This is from the top, Hank."

"Then why isn't one of them here? Why send you?"

"It's a courtesy call. I asked for the job."

Hank looked over at him and frowned. The past lay between them like a minefield.

"People are wondering. You quitting so soon after the job, a job that apparently you didn't want. Or complete," Cameron said. "There's talk that you might have been seeing her. Romantically."

Hank let out a curse.

"How else, they say, can you explain the fact that she's alive after you were told to kill her?"

Hank laughed and downed his drink. He couldn't explain it. But there was no doubt in his mind that the woman in the photograph was Rena. "What is it you want me to say?"

Cameron shook his head. "The agency just wants clarification that it is Rena—and an explanation of why she is still alive and working again for the other side."

Chapter Seven

The first time Meredith Foster saw Whitehorse, Montana, she wondered what had possessed her husband to go there of all places.

He could have gone anywhere in the world when he took off with his suitcase and his dreams of freedom. It showed a distinct lack of imagination on John's part that he would come to this little isolated town in the middle of nowhere.

Had he lost his mind?

Considering what had forced her to drive to Whitehorse she had assumed he had. And yet she'd been thankful the town was small. It had certainly made her job easier.

She'd gone straight to the Shady Rest Motel.

The bell over the door had jangled as she'd entered. The air conditioner had hummed in the window while a television droned somewhere in the back. There'd been a crash, loud words and then a child crying, another whining.

Impatiently Meredith had gone over to the door, opened and closed it again. This time when the bell jangled a fiftysomething woman had appeared. "May I help you?"

"I certainly hope so," Meredith had said and considered the woman and the best approach—money or tears—to get what she wanted.

Tears had worked like a charm. The poor betrayed wife could always get the sympathy—and the help.

The motel manager had seen John Foster with a local young blond woman from a questionable family in Old Town.

"Her name?" Meredith had asked. "I just want to talk to her. Make sure she leaves my husband alone."

The woman behind the desk had nodded. "Charlotte. Charlotte Evans."

To Meredith's surprise, it had been harder to get information at the restaurant where her husband had gone for dinner.

Charlotte Evans had been a waitress there. No one remembered a guest named John Foster. Charlotte might have waited on him. But the owner, a woman named Laci Cavanaugh, hadn't been willing to provide any information.

"I just want to know why my husband *doubled* his bill as a tip?" Meredith had demanded.

"I wouldn't know, Mrs. Foster. Why don't you ask your husband?"

Meredith had left in a huff. Neither money nor tears had swayed the indomitable Laci Cavanaugh.

Meredith had left shocked that Charlotte Evans was only eighteen. The fool. No wonder John had come home with his tail tucked between his legs. He was damned lucky the girl hadn't lied about her age—or he'd be in jail right now.

She'd felt such a wave of disgust for her husband that

for a few moments, she'd thought about returning home and tossing his butt out.

But common sense had reigned. Charlotte Evans was a nobody and certainly not a threat to Meredith's marriage.

And yet Meredith had known she couldn't leave town—all ten blocks square of it—without seeing this young woman.

The downtown sat adjacent to the railroad tracks, like a lot of towns along the Hi-Line, from what she could gather.

As Meredith had waited in her car along the quiet street outside the Cut and Curl, where she'd been told Charlotte Evans worked, she hadn't been able to imagine living in such a small town.

At quitting time, several women—who obviously all worked there, since they wore matching pink smocks—had come out of the shop. Finally Charlotte Evans had emerged alone and walked to an old blue car parked at the curb.

From what Meredith had heard about the girl, she would have known Charlotte anywhere. What had shocked her was that Charlotte looked younger than eighteen.

What *had* John been thinking? He could have had a daughter her age.

It made Meredith sick to think of John with the blonde, and she'd wondered if waking up next to the girl and realizing how young she was wasn't what had sent John running home.

Disgusted, but not worried about this eighteen-year-old taking her husband, Meredith had hurriedly driven through town, anxious to get home. But on the edge of town she'd noticed that she needed gas.

In this part of Montana, the towns were so far apart she'd had to take advantage of stations along the way or run out of gas in the middle of nowhere on a highway with little traffic.

She'd pulled into a convenience store called Packy's, filled up and gone in for a cup of coffee to keep her awake for the three-hour drive home.

As she'd been waiting to pay, she'd recognized the two women she'd seen coming out of the beauty shop only minutes before Charlotte Evans. The two had their heads together as they waited in line.

Meredith moved closer when she heard one of the women mention Charlotte. She'd listened to the two discuss some big announcement Charlotte had made that day at work.

"Do you think she really did it on purpose?" the one had whispered to the other.

"That's what she said. It's just disgusting even if she didn't, getting knocked up by some old married guy from out of town. She says they were both drunk and that all she remembers is that his name was John."

The one young woman had broken up in giggles. "She got pregnant by a *john*."

Meredith had stood rooted to the floor until finally she heard the clerk call, "Ma'am, can I help you?" She didn't remember paying for her gas and coffee or walking out into the hot afternoon sun to her car.

John. The asinine girl had told these women that she had purposely gotten pregnant by a man from out of town named John?

Meredith had driven a few miles out of town before

she'd had to pull over and, physically ill, had retched beside the road. She'd tried to still the panic. The girl had set John up, purposely getting pregnant by the fool so she could…what?

The realization had hit her like a fist, and she'd had to clutch the side of the car as she'd bent over again with another spasm.

There was only one reason: extortion. Soon Charlotte Evans would be contacting John, telling him about the baby, demanding money. Or, worse, marriage?

If John found out, he would do the "right" thing. He'd always wanted children. Meredith hadn't. Even her father and father-in-law would support John, at least in making sure he took care of his child—especially if the child was a son.

She abhorred the thought of money that belonged to her going to some bastard child and his whore mother. But she knew there was nothing she could do if the foolish girl decided to contact John. The one thing she could not let happen was lose anything that belonged to her because of this mess.

Meredith had left Whitehorse frantic with worry. By the time she'd reached home, she'd calmed down enough to think rationally. There was only one thing to do.

She would have to get pregnant—and right away.

"CLARIFICATION?" Hank demanded as he watched Cameron take a drink to one of the leather chairs.

"You can't blame them, Hank."

Like hell he couldn't. He tried to calm down. "What is it they want me to do?" Hank asked, fearing the answer.

"Nothing. We just needed confirmation."

"And clarification."

Cameron shrugged. "They'll take what they get."

He stared at Cameron, too shocked to speak for a moment. "That's it? They aren't demanding I fix this? Or, hell, putting out a hit on me?"

Cameron laughed and shook his head. "Like I said, there's talk. They'd like to know how this happened, but as far as taking any action…" He shook his head again.

Hank glanced toward the darkened window and felt a sudden chill. He remembered another dark night and what he'd thought was a confirmed kill.

He could pretty much guess how it had happened. Rena had expected the hit. Someone had leaked that the agency was onto her. She had set him up. It was that simple. And that complex.

Hank said as much to Cameron, who simply nodded.

"That's the way I figured it. I'll be sure I put that in my report," Cam said. He finished his drink and reached for the folder with the photographers inside. "My job is done, then."

Hank had been so surprised by Cam's visit he hadn't been thinking clearly. But he was now. "You could have sent the photographs electronically and saved yourself the trip."

"And missed being verbally abused by you?" Cam shook his head. "Don't worry. You're still a legend with the agency. This doesn't change that."

Hank let out a curse. "I wasn't worried about my legend status, and you know it." He had to admit it was good to see Cam. He studied his once best friend and realized maybe he hadn't lost his edge. "You think she's going to come after me. That's why you came here yourself."

"It crossed my mind and a few other minds," Cam said.

Hank began to laugh. "You were *worried* about me."

"Don't let it go to your head."

Even with their difference in age, there'd been a time they were closer than brothers. But that was before Rena, before she went to the other side, before Hank was ordered to kill her.

"Just watch your back," Cameron said as he tucked the folder under his arm and pocketed the magnifying glass.

"Where are you staying?"

"I'm not. I'm driving back to Billings tonight so I can catch an early flight out. If you didn't live in such a God-forsaken place…"

It was three hours to the closest large airport, with miles between towns.

"That's what I love about it up here," Hank said. "They call it 'the big open.' Have you ever seen a bigger sky or felt as small and insignificant?"

Cameron laughed. "You actually *like* it here."

He nodded. "Just one question," he said as Cam got ready to leave. "They aren't hoping to use me as bait to catch her, are they?"

Cameron shook his head almost sadly. "You wanted it that way when you quit the agency. Said you didn't want to see any spooks for any reason."

Hank laughed again. He didn't buy it for a minute. "I know what they're up to. They think my pride will force me to track her down and finish the job. My last job. My perfect record. They think I miss this crap?" He sobered. "I'm done with that life, Cam. I can't kill anymore."

Cameron smiled. "Take care, Hank. I have no idea what

you're doing out here in the middle of nowhere, but it really was great seeing you again."

"I wish I could say the same," Hank said, but he reached for his friend's hand and pulled him into a quick hug. "Watch for deer along the highway. That's the biggest threat we have up here."

"You just keep telling yourself that," Cameron said.

Hank watched him hike down the back road to where he must have stashed his vehicle and felt sorry about the way things had turned out. But then, that wasn't anything new, was it? Cameron had saved his life—and taken it from him by getting him into the agency.

Closing the blinds, Hank walked back to the bar and thought about Rena, wondering how long it would be before he saw her again.

With Rena on the loose, he was a walking target. The last thing he wanted was Arlene to be anywhere near those crosshairs.

MEREDITH THREW A surprise dinner party not long after her return from Whitehorse to announce her good news.

She'd waited until everyone was seated and, in the glow of the candles and fine china, announced, "I'm pregnant."

In the shocked silence, it was John's expression that she'd wanted to see the most. He knew that she'd never wanted children, abhorred the idea.

He'd gone deathly pale, his dark eyes wide as the charger under his dinner plate. Then he'd met her gaze and held it, the look in his eyes hardening to flint.

Then they'd both known that she had him right where she wanted him.

"Congratulations!" her father had boomed into the stunned silence. "I, for one, couldn't be happier."

Her mother had smiled over at her, a triumphant twinkle in her eye as she gave her daughter a slight nod.

Meredith had kept a happy smile on her face all through dinner, but she'd worried that this would backfire on her and she would end up with a child she didn't want and John gone.

When she'd mentioned this to her mother later in the kitchen, her mother had given her a rueful smile. "You know John. He has the spine of a jellyfish. That's why you married him to begin with. He might leave you, but never if there is a child. John is brought to tears at the sight of kittens."

"I hope you're right, Mother."

"A woman does what she has to do. Haven't you learned that yet?"

Back in the dining room after dessert, her father-in-law had raised his glass in another toast. Meredith had noticed that her mother-in-law had been watching John from the stony expression on her face, her sentiments had been with her son—and didn't include a grandchild. At least not with Meredith.

She'd once overheard John's mother tell a friend, "I worry for John. Meredith is so…headstrong."

The friend had laughed and said, "Headstrong? And as warm as a glacier. I can't for the life of me understand what John sees in her."

"I tried to talk him out of marrying her, but his father…" That's when Fran Foster had looked up and seen Meredith and known that she'd heard *every* word. Their eyes had locked, and Meredith had let her know with just one look that she would always hate her.

After her announcement, Meredith had raised her water glass, wishing it were wine, and tried her best to look demure. Her hatred of Fran Foster was nothing compared to what she felt for John. He'd forced her into this. She planned to make his life a living hell.

"Thank you," Meredith had said after John senior's toast. "John and I couldn't be happier. Isn't that right, sweetheart?"

John being John had nodded. "We couldn't be happier."

ARLENE WAS GETTING ready for bed when she noticed there was a message from Sheriff Carter Jackson.

She dialed his home number at once, fearing the worst.

He answered on the second ring. "Arlene, I just wanted to ask if you'd heard from Charlotte."

She had to sit on her bed, her legs were so weak. "Yes. That is, she called and sent a note. We found her car in a gully not far from here. She says she's with the father of her baby."

If the sheriff heard the hesitation in her voice, he didn't react to it. "Good," he said. "I'd hoped that was all it was. I'm going to be out of the office for the rest of the week, then two weeks on my honeymoon…."

"Your wedding. Yes."

"But if you need me—"

"No. I'm fine."

He seemed to hesitate. "Well, one of the deputies will be here, should anything arise."

"Yes." She thanked him for his call and hung up.

Exhausted, she crawled into bed and was almost asleep when she heard the deep throb of a motorcycle. She sat up as the noise grew louder, then died away to the chirp of crickets again.

Charlotte?

She jumped out of bed, pulling her robe around her as she headed for the front door. She stopped abruptly at the sound of a heavy tread on the porch steps.

Peering out the window, she saw the large shape of a man stop at the door and raise his hand to knock.

She opened the door to Charlotte's former boyfriend, bracing herself for the worst.

"Don't go off on me," Lucas Bronson said, holding up both hands. He wore black leather pants and jacket, a red bandanna tied around his dark hair. "I come in peace."

Arlene glared at him. "I thought we saw the last of you." Lucas had been in and out of Charlotte's life since she was fourteen. In and out of trouble during that same time, Lucas was the last person Arlene wanted to see, especially now. "Do you realize how late it is?"

Lucas smiled. He was a good-looking young man a year older than Bo. He came from a broken family—but then, few families weren't broken, Arlene thought.

"I know it's late," he said. "I just need to see Charlotte. It's important."

"Yo, Lucas, my man!" Bo said from behind her as he pushed past to shake hands with the biker. "Hey, it's good to see you."

"Bo, please go back to bed. I need to speak to Lucas," Arlene said.

Bo shot her a look, no doubt surprised by the calmness he heard in her tone. "What brings you back, man?"

"I need to see Charlotte," Lucas said, craning to look past them into the house. "I hate to wake her, but it really is important."

"I'm afraid—" Arlene began, but Bo cut her off.

"She took off, Luke. Nobody knows where she is."

Lucas looked as if he'd been punched. "No way! She's got to be really pregnant by now."

"Eight months," Arlene said, realizing as she said it that Charlotte had originally lied to her about how far along she was. She hadn't been but a couple of months when she'd told Arlene she was four months along.

Lucas was shaking his head. "She's got to be closer to nine months, since she's carrying my kid."

"*What?*" Arlene demanded.

"Didn't she tell you?" Then he seemed to realize how ridiculous that was. "Sorry, I guess she probably didn't. It's *my* baby."

"How do you know that?" Arlene demanded.

"She told me she was pregnant before I left."

"But you left *anyway?*"

He had the good sense to look ashamed. "But I'm back *now*. I'm going to marry her."

Arlene groaned. "Did Charlotte know this?"

"We talked about it. She wasn't real keen on it. But I know I can talk her into it."

Arlene tried to shake away the cobwebs in her brain. This didn't make any sense. "I got a call from her saying she was with the baby's father and they were making a new life for themselves."

Lucas shook his head. "No way. Unless it's that old guy she said she was going to get to pay for all her medical expenses."

"Old guy?" Arlene echoed. Old as in *thirty*something John Foster?

Lucas ducked his head, realizing he'd said too much.

"Tell me. My daughter is missing. If you know anything…"

"She bedded some old guy. They didn't…you know. She drugged him and made him think—"

"I get the picture," Arlene snapped thinking if Charlotte was here, she'd ring her neck.

"Wow," Bo said, sounding impressed by his sister's antics.

"I thought I told you to go back to bed," Arlene snapped at her son. "Lucas, you go wherever it is you go. But if you hear anything from Charlotte—"

"I'll let you know. It's weird. I haven't heard from her in several days. I thought maybe she already had the baby."

Several days? Charlotte had been in contact with him? Why, Arlene groaned, was this news to her? "Was she threatening to run away the last time you heard from her?"

"No. She said she'd changed her mind about, you know, hitting the old man up for money," Lucas said. "She was thinking about giving the baby up for adoption. That's when I realized I had to get back here and stop her."

Great, Arlene thought. Charlotte actually had been listening to reason. Maybe there was cause for hope. Or not, she thought, remembering that Lucas had come home to stop her. And knowing Charlotte…

Back in the house, Arlene waited until the sound of the motorcycle faded before she picked up the phone and started to dial Hank's number.

She put the phone back. She wasn't going to be able to get back to sleep and she desperately needed someone to talk to, but she didn't want to do this over the phone. With luck, Hank would still be up. He'd told her once that he was a night owl.

She quickly dressed and drove to his ranch. While she'd never been inside, she'd seen the house from the road when it had belonged to some corporation that only used it a couple of weeks a year.

The lights were on, she saw with relief.

By the time she'd parked her pickup in front of the huge house and gotten out, Hank was standing on the porch, a dark, large silhouette against the lights inside.

The way he stood made her hesitate. Maybe this hadn't been such a good idea after all. It had been impulsive. Hadn't she learned in the past where that kind of behavior got her? Maybe her children had inherited this behavior from her.

She stopped partway to the house. "Hank?"

"What's going on?" he asked. He sounded as if he'd been drinking. Yes, this had been a bad idea.

"I…that is, I thought you might still be up. I hope you don't mind me coming over." She moved toward the porch. "Charlotte's old boyfriend just stopped by. It seems she told him *he* is the baby's father."

"Do you believe him?" Hank asked as she climbed the wide steps to where he stood. She saw that he had a half-finished drink in his hand.

"I think it's possible." She told Hank about Charlotte's plan. "Apparently she drugged John Foster and made him think they slept together so she could later get money out of him. At least that's the story she told Lucas, her biker boyfriend."

Hank nodded but said nothing. He hadn't invited her inside, either. Clearly he wasn't happy to see her.

"I shouldn't have come by so late," she said. "I'm sorry."

"No," he said. "It's just a lot to take in."

She'd warned him that her family was a train wreck, but it just got worse each day. Hank hadn't signed on for this. She felt guilty. Worse, she'd known it was only a matter of time before he tired of the drama. She certainly had.

When he'd signed up for her rural Meet-A-Mate Internet dating service, he'd said he was retired, looking for someone to spend quality time with, like traveling around the world. He'd just wanted someone to date a few times, have some fun with—not to get roped into their problems.

"I should go," she said and turned to leave.

"Arlene." He seemed at a loss for words as she turned back, and suddenly she was scared of what he would say when he found them.

"I was going to call you," he said finally. "I think we need to take a step back. It's just that things have been happening so fast with us…."

She felt her heart drop. "You don't have to explain. I understand."

"It's not *you.*"

Her smile hurt.

"Arlene, when I met you I thought I was ready to start dating, but—"

"My service will find you someone more compatible," she said quickly. "Unless you want to cancel your membership. I'll be happy to refund your money."

"No. That is, I don't want to date anyone else. But I don't want you to lose money on me. I won't break my contract."

"I don't need your money." She warned herself not to say any more, but the words came out sounding as painful as they felt. "Or your sympathy. Isn't that what these have been—pity dates?"

"You're wrong. I thought I could do this, but…"

She turned to leave.

"Arlene!" He swore. "I've handled this so damned poorly. Won't you at least hear me out?"

"I hear you just fine," she called back to him as she hurried to her pickup. She started the engine and backed up, fighting the pain, the disappointment, the hurt.

He was still standing on the porch as she drove away.

She wouldn't cry.

She.

Would.

Not.

Cry.

Chapter Eight

The next morning Arlene Evans did something completely out of character. She got up, showered, dressed and drove into Whitehorse without making her bed, without making her son breakfast, without cleaning up her house or starting a load or two of clothes in the washer.

Twenty minutes later she was sitting in the Cut and Curl, so nervous she could barely contain herself.

"You're sure?" Linsey asked, looking more worried than Arlene felt. Clearly all the women in the shop had been shocked to see Arlene walk in—and nervous. "I could just trim a little—"

"No. Cut it off." Arlene closed her eyes at the sound of the scissors. She felt the slight tug at the end of her long, thick hair. She squeezed her eyes shut tighter, feeling as if she was losing more than hair. There was a literal attachment to her hair, a familiarity, a constant that she wasn't sure she could part with.

Too late.

She felt the brush of fingers next to her ear, the cool feel of her wet hair, the whisper of the comb, then the snap of the scissors again and again.

She kept her eyes closed, let her thoughts run. The anger she'd felt at Hank seemed to leave her like the long strands of her hair. She felt herself changing and realized it had been gradual for some time now.

Ever since he'd walked into her life. It was as if he'd started something that couldn't be stopped. He'd been the catalyst. But even with him gone from her life, she couldn't stop what was happening to her.

What's more, she didn't hear her mother's voice in her head, berating her, anymore.

And was it just her imagination or did her head feel almost weightless?

She heard Linsey sweeping up the hair around the chair, then finally a timid question, "Want to take a look, Mrs. Evans?"

"Arlene," she said. "Please call me Arlene." Slowly she opened her eyes. Her hair was still damp, chin-length but layered so it fell in soft curls around her face.

She stared at herself in the mirror. A stranger. No, she thought, tears welling in her eyes. She *knew* this woman. This was the woman she could have been. Should have been. This woman had something the old Arlene never had—a glimmer of hope in her eyes.

"You hate it," Linsey said, taking a step back.

"No," Arlene said quickly. "I love it." She smiled, surprised how the cut seemed to soften her face, even her voice. "I *love* it."

Linsey breathed a relieved sigh and smiled. "It looks good on you. You look so…different."

The other women in the shop added their approval, as well.

Arlene nodded. She felt different. "Thank you."

Linsey beamed. Clearly she'd been worried.

Arlene paid her, giving her a nice tip, and stepped out of the shop, lighter, freer somehow. Amazing what a hair cut could do. If she'd known this, she would have gotten one a lot sooner.

She smiled at the thought because it was so unlikely. That old Arlene Evans would have hated this haircut. That Arlene had spent years hiding behind her hair.

She listened for her mother's two cents worth.

Not a word.

She smiled, feeling freer than she had ever imagined she could feel…except for that little ache in her heart where Hank had been.

A WARM DRY WIND blew across the rolling hills keeling over the tall green grass. Hank rode his horse toward the horizon, dust churning up behind him.

In the distance the Little Rockies met the sky in a ragged dark line of deep purple. Above him a hawk soared in all that blue, and only a wisp of clouds scudded along high overhead.

As he rode, he could almost imagine the endless herds of buffalo that had rumbled over this land before him. Before barbed wire. Before the white man.

As a boy, he'd never dreamed of anything like this. Not the land. Nor the ranch. Or even the horse beneath him.

Hell, he'd never dreamed at all. As young as he'd been, he'd seen his future in the dirty streets, in the faces of the poor and disheartened. Cameron had rescued him from that urban squalor. And Hank had blamed him ever since.

You're not angry at Cameron. You're furious with yourself and you know damned well why.

He'd been mentally kicking himself all morning. Usually he could lose himself on horseback as if transported to another time, another life in this immense country.

But not today.

All he could think about was Arlene. He hated the way he'd left things last night.

All his fault. He should never have signed up for the dating service, let alone asked her out. Had he really thought he could put his past behind him? A past like his?

There were no second chances.

And yet, even as he thought it, he rebelled at the idea. The moment he'd seen Arlene that day in the café he'd been filled with a desire to start over. Maybe he had asked her out on impulse. Certainly she had tugged at his heartstrings.

And maybe it had originally been a pity date, just as she'd accused him. He'd seen himself in her and felt sorry for them both. How pitiful was that?

He'd been lonely. He'd wanted someone to share this part of his life with. He'd sensed that Arlene needed a second chance as much as he did.

What had he thought? That he'd find an uncomplicated woman? As if there was such a thing. But Arlene definitely wasn't that.

She was the most complex woman he'd ever met. Maybe that had been part of the fascination, as well. He'd never met anyone like her. She'd *lived*. Just as he had. And they both had the scars to prove it.

The difference was, his old baggage could get him

killed. Arlene thought she'd messed up her life? She had no idea the kind of trouble he could bring to her.

He did what he had to do. Walked away. For her sake.

You always were so full of bull, Hank Monroe.

He swore under his breath. Okay, maybe Arlene did scare him. Being with her would be complicated. She made him feel things he'd hoped never to feel again. He'd wanted someone to spend time with, not someone he might fall in love with.

Arlene made him want to step up and be a better man. When he was with her he felt so deeply....

He drew his horse up as a spooked herd of antelope thundered down a sandy-bluffed draw, their color blending perfectly with their surroundings.

"So what the hell are you going to do?" Hank asked himself, his words sailing off on the wind.

He could try to outrun his past. Or he could stay and fight. It was ironic, in a way, that he had moved to a part of Montana that had been lawless until as late as the early 1900s. At least back then you could tell the good guys from the bad even when they weren't wearing their hats.

His horse shuddered under him and took an impatient step as if to say, *Make a decision.*

It wasn't that he hadn't known until that moment what he wanted. He just hadn't admitted it.

With a curse, he turned his horse back toward the ranch. He'd lived by one rule his whole life: There were some things worth fighting for even against the odds.

This life here in this part of Montana was worth fighting for. So was Arlene.

Not that it didn't scare the hell out of him. But he'd

made up his mind. He'd tell Arlene everything. He'd understand if she wanted nothing to do with him given his past—and the fact that a hired killer might be coming after him.

After taking care of his horse, he hurried into the house from the barn to answer his ringing phone, thinking it might be Arlene.

He didn't reach his office in time. The answering machine picked up.

"Hank." Cameron's voice.

He felt a chill shudder through him.

"Good news. You've been approved for digital TV. And that little problem we had with your credit—that's been taken care of. So it's all locked up. Nothing to worry about. Hope that makes your day." There was a click on the line. The answering machine hummed a while longer and then fell silent.

Rena. They'd caught her.

Now all he had to do was find Arlene and hope she'd give him another chance.

ARLENE CAUGHT HER reflection in the window as she headed for her pickup and felt a jolt as it took her a moment to even recognize herself.

She heard a car door open and close and saw Hank coming toward her from across the street.

She didn't know what to feel after last night. But as hard as she tried, she couldn't crush the pleasure that sprang up inside her at just the sight of him.

He smiled, taking in her hair, her face. The tenderness of his gaze was almost her undoing. "Hello, beautiful," he said.

She couldn't help but laugh. Not her usual donkey laugh, this one soft, throaty. His good mood was contagious. So different from the man on his porch last night. What had brought about this change?

She'd promised herself that when she saw him again she wouldn't allow herself to feel anything. That she would go back to being impervious, back to the woman who wouldn't show her hurt even if it killed her.

But there was no going back. Her pleasure showed in her face. She could feel it. Just like her vulnerability. She had no defenses against this man.

"I'm sorry about last night," Hank said quickly. "I need to tell you what's been going on with me if you'll give me the chance. I came to find you. Mind taking a ride?"

"You really don't need to explain," Arlene said, fearing the explanation could be more painful than even what had been said last night.

He stepped to her so quickly she didn't have a chance to react. His arm encircled her waist. He pulled her to him, his mouth dropping to hers.

The kiss took her even more by surprise. It was filled with passion and yearning and possession.

And when it ended, he pulled back to look in her eyes. "Please give me a second chance."

She could do nothing more than nod, her heart a thunder in her chest as he slipped her hand into his large one and they walked across the street like that. She knew that Linsey and the others would be watching from the window, speculating, but she didn't care. His kiss had warmed her all over, and his hand felt so good, warm, lightly callused, strong.

He drove her out to his ranch, touching her cheek or her hand or her arm occasionally on the way, as if afraid she might bolt.

She'd heard about the house on the rumor mill, but the only local she knew who'd been inside since Hank had bought it was Claudia Nicholson, who cleaned for him.

"I know it's too big," he said as he shoved open the door and stepped back to let her enter. "I'm not sure what I was thinking."

She looked around the massive living room and kitchen and thought about what Bo had said to her. Hank definitely had money. Did the government pay this well?

"Would you like something to drink?" he offered.

She shook her head, concentrating on breathing. Difficult this close to him. She could smell his clean, freshly showered scent. He wore jeans that on him looked sexier than any cowboy's south forty she'd ever seen.

"I want to be honest with you," he said, stepping to her. "I'm crazy about you. Last night I panicked because there was a problem with my former occupation, a loose end that— Oh, hell, a rogue agent I thought was dead who apparently isn't. But I just found out that she's been caught."

"She?" Arlene had to ask.

He nodded. "It's a long story and I don't want to talk about the past. I want…" His gaze locked with hers. "I want you." He let out a small laugh. "Hell, Arlene, you're all I think about. I'm asking you to take a risk here."

A shiver skated the length of her spine at his words. Take a risk? She smiled at that. He had no idea how much of a risk she was taking. Her heart, her hope, the chance of losing this woman she felt herself becoming before she even had a chance to know her.

She was scared. Not of this man's past. But of the future. Especially the immediate future.

I want you.

If she stayed here, she knew they would end up making love. Or at least she hoped so.

Had she ever made love? She had three grown children, but she knew what Floyd had done to her certainly was nothing like in books or movies. Not only that, she hadn't been with a man in… She couldn't even remember the last time Floyd had touched her.

"I'm not afraid," she lied, her voice breaking.

He smiled. "I can see that."

She touched his cheek with the tips of her fingers. That first step, she thought, is always the hardest. But she took it, closing the distance between them. Her pulse thrummed as she cupped his face in her palms and kissed him. He drew her close and she melted into him, knowing there was no turning back now.

HANK COULD FEEL Arlene trembling and warned himself to take it slow. He couldn't remember the last time he'd been with a woman. But, fortunately, it was a lot like riding a bike. And this woman made his desire flare and burst into flame. He brushed a lock of her hair back from her cheek. "I like your haircut. It suits you."

Her smile was shy. "I don't know myself anymore."

"I do," he said and kissed her. She came to him, her body softening against his. He saw her arousal in the warm brown of her eyes, flickering heat that flashed and fired as he touched her. A brush of fingers along her slim throat. The glimmer of a touch to her lips with his tongue. The gentle press of his palm hot against her back as he drew her in.

She moaned softly at his touch, fanning his own desire. He slipped the top button on her shirt, his fingers brushing the tender skin at her throat. She shivered as he slipped the next button free, exposing the top of her bra. He saw her throat work as she swallowed. In her eyes, fear mixed with excitement, with desire, with raw need.

The bra was white, the rounded curves of her breasts just as white. His fingertips skimmed over her tender bare skin, the flesh rippling with goose bumps ahead of his touch.

Slowly he opened her shirt and slipped it off her shoulders, letting it fall to the floor. She swallowed again. His gaze locked with hers as he ran his hands over her bare shoulders and down her arms. He could see the hardened nipples of her breasts pressed against the white fabric of her bra.

He reached behind her, unhooked the bra and freed her breasts. As the fabric brushed the hard tips, she made a sound deep in her throat that skyrocketed his own need. He'd never wanted a woman as badly as he wanted this one.

ARLENE FELT WEAK, her legs like water as Hank took her full breasts in his big hands, branding her flesh with heat. Her nipples hardened to aching peaks as his gaze traveled over the swell of her breasts.

She let out a moan, her head falling back as he lowered

his mouth to lathe the dark nipples with his tongue. Heat shot to her center. Her insides felt molten and she thought she would die if he didn't take her—and soon.

"Hank," she said on a breath. "Please."

He cupped her bottom with his hands, lifting her off the floor as he carried her to the couch of soft, deep leather. She sank into it, Hank beside her. At the touch of a button, blinds dropped over the windows in a whisper.

His kisses were slow and sensuous. She felt the heat begin to build even higher, a slow, steady flame that licked along her nerve endings.

In the cool, dim light, her fingers worked quickly to remove his shirt, her palms itching to feel the warmth of his chest. With each button freed she discovered tanned, smooth flesh lightly sprinkled with honey-brown hair that narrowed to a vee at the top of his jeans.

As she spread his shirt wide, he dragged her on top of him, her breasts pressed into his hard chest. She heard his sharp intake of breath, felt the hardness of him, the soft tenderness of his mouth as he kissed her.

They wriggled out of their jeans as they rolled around on the huge couch like teenagers, grappling and groping.

Hank let out a chuckle as, finally naked, he pulled her against him so they were lying side by side, facing each other. "You feel so damned good, Arlene Evans."

She felt his fingers slip between her thighs. She let out a small surprised, pleased cry as he touched her. Her heart began to pound, her breasts ached from her hardened nipples and, against her will, her hips began to move with the motion of his fingers.

"Hank." The word came out on a gasp. "Hank!"

The feeling rocked through her, blinding her, shocking her, liberating her.

He rolled on top of her, his breath tickling her neck as he trailed kisses over her jawline to her mouth. His eyes locked with hers and she saw recognition in his gaze. His look softened, and she felt embarrassed and ashamed that this was the first time she'd ever felt this. All those wasted years.

But almost at once the feeling vanished. She had a lot of years to make up for. Starting right now. He raised himself over her and she wrapped her arms around his neck.

She lifted her hips to meet him, wanting him inside her, needing him inside her.

And then he filled her, making her catch her breath. She rocked against him, caught up in the rhythm of lovemaking for the first time.

That building inside her started again. The beginning of a roller-coaster ride, the climbing up, up, up until she thought she couldn't go any higher or she would start screaming. And then she reached the top, Hank right there with her, and they plummeted down the other side in a breathtaking release of pleasure beyond her wildest dreams.

They lay together, locked in each others arms, panting and laughing and gazing longingly at one another.

"Wow," he said as he rose up on one elbow to look down at her.

And suddenly she felt shy and a little embarrassed as his gaze took in the length of her. She froze as she saw him focus on her cesarean scar and quickly tried to cover it with her arm, but he stopped her, moving her arm aside as he sat up.

Then, to her amazement, he leaned down and trailed a line of kisses across the ridge of the scar.

When he raised his head, his eyes locked with hers. She reached for him, cradling his head in her hands as she pulled him onto her and kissed him.

She'd suspected she was falling in love with Hank Monroe. Now she knew she was.

Chapter Nine

Arlene woke in Hank's big bed to the smell of bacon. For a moment she just lay there, luxuriating in the cool, silken feel of the sheets and in the small homey sounds coming from the kitchen, reliving the long afternoon.

Her cheeks flushed at the memory. The man had been insatiable—and the things he'd done to her! Floyd had never! During their marriage, he would come in from the field, lie down beside her in bed at night and, after a chaste kiss on her cheek, climb on her and huff and puff until he was sated, then he would roll over and go to sleep, and she would lie there until he began to snore.

She would rise, wash up, put on a clean nightgown and go back to bed, where it would take her forever to get to sleep.

She'd never imagined the kind of responses a man like Hank could elicit from her body. *Her* body! She'd never been so wanton. Or so satisfied. Her body felt molten inside, reshaped by fire.

"Hello."

She looked up to see Hank standing in the doorway.

He smiled at her and strode over to the bed to lean down and kiss her.

"What time is it?" she asked, glancing toward the window. The sky was still light.

"A little after four in the afternoon. I hope you're hungry. I'm making us bacon cheeseburgers."

"Oh, that sounds heavenly." She sat up, the sheets falling away from her bare breasts.

"If you keep that up, I'll burn the bacon," he warned, his voice low and laced with fresh longing.

Her own desire sparked, but she pulled the sheet over her breasts, feeling the need for a shower. She glanced toward the bathroom.

"Help yourself to whatever you need," he called over his shoulder as he left the room to get back to the kitchen and the bacon.

In the bathroom, she turned on the shower and stepped in. The warm water washed over her skin, reminding her of Hank's hands, his mouth, his body. She shuddered and hurriedly showered.

As she stepped out, her skin flushed, she caught her reflection in the mirror—and was taken aback. She'd completely forgotten about her haircut.

Smiling at her reflection, she fluffed up the wet curls, pleased with the look. Just plain pleased. It felt strange to feel this way, and for just an instant she almost let worry suck the life back out of her. She'd worried about everything under the sun all her life. It felt good to just feel good for a while.

When she opened the bathroom door, she saw that Hank had left her one of his clean shirts and a pair of his shorts.

She put them on and, enticed by the smell of bacon cheese-burgers, padded barefoot down the hall feeling decadent.

She found Hank in the kitchen. He looked surprisingly at home even in such a large commercial kitchen. He handed her a beer and motioned to the table by the window.

Arlene had never had a man cook for her before. She realized as she sat down across from him that he'd provided her with a lot of firsts since they'd met. It amazed her that a woman her age, with three grown children, could have experienced so little. Until now.

They talked and laughed and ate as if they were both starving after their morning and most of the afternoon. She was just getting up to clear the table when the phone rang down the hall.

"I need to get that. Just leave those dishes," Hank called back to her as he hurried down the hall.

She couldn't just leave the dirty dishes. Carrying them over to the sink, she rinsed them and put them in the dishwasher. She had just finished when he came back into the room.

One look at his face and she knew it was bad news.

"What?" she asked on a breath.

"You know I've been looking into Charlotte's disappearance—"

"I forgot to tell you. I got a note from her saying she was fine." Arlene rushed to where she'd dropped her shoulder bag, driven by a need to believe her daughter was all right. She quickly dug through and brought out the envelope. "It's her handwriting. She's fine. She…" Arlene stopped, halted by the look on his face. *"No."*

"As far as I know, Charlotte is still fine," he said, coming to her and drawing her into him. "But I don't think she left of her own free will."

Arlene pulled back. "Why would you say—"

"There were no fingerprints on the steering wheel of Charlotte's car," he said.

She stared at him. "But the motor grease…"

"Whoever pushed the car into the ravine was wearing gloves. Latex gloves. The lab was able to pick up some of the residue from the gloves."

Arlene was shaking her head. "Why would they…?" She turned from him, biting down on her lip. "But Charlotte called, sent me a note…"

"From what you've told me about Charlotte, letting you know so you won't worry isn't like her," he said quietly behind her. "Am I wrong?"

"No." The word came out on a sob.

"The good news is that someone got her to make the call and write the note so she is all right," he said. "But there is something else. After you told me about her boyfriend Lucas?"

She turned. "Yes?"

"I did some checking. If Lucas is telling the truth, based on when you said he left town and what he told you, then Charlotte is closer to nine months pregnant."

"Yes, but…" She understood before he said the words.

"If the person who took her doesn't realize that, they won't be expecting her to give birth yet. They might not be ready when the baby comes."

"The baby? They want the baby?" Arlene cried breaking free to pace around the kitchen. "But Charlotte…what about—" The words died in her throat as she turned to look at him. "We have to find her."

He reached for Arlene, dragging her into his arms, holding her tight. "We'll find her. Get dressed. We need to get going."

She pulled back. "Where…?"

"Let's start with the local gas stations. There's a chance that if Meredith was in Whitehorse, someone will remember her. If they saw her with Charlotte, then we will have something to take to the sheriff."

HANK DROVE THEM into town and hit the three gas stations. At the first two, no one recalled a woman matching Meredith Foster's description. Fortunately Meredith Foster would have stood out in Whitehorse.

They hit pay dirt at the gas station on the road south out of town, Packy's.

"I remember a woman like you described," said the cute blond clerk. "I could tell she wanted to pay at the pump and was put out that she had to come inside."

"Was there anyone with her?" Arlene asked hopefully.

"Not that I know of."

Hank tried to hide his disappointment. "What time of the day was it?"

The blonde thought for a moment then started to shake her head but stopped. "No, wait a minute. I *do* remember. I was eating a piece of pizza for lunch behind the counter when she came in. I put it down to wait on her, but I remember her glancing at it as if I was committing a national offense."

That sounded like Meredith.

"Other than gas, did she purchase anything else?"

"Nope. That was it."

Meredith had gotten gas on Friday *before* Charlotte had left home for her doctor's appointment and had not been seen again. So there was no way Charlotte would have been in the SUV. No eyewitnesses. No evidence except circumstantial.

"I forgot to ask you what she was driving," Hank said.

The clerk thought for a moment. "Silver. Can't tell you what make, but it was one of those fancy SUVs."

A silver SUV. Like the one Arlene had seen drive by the house on more than one occasion.

As they were leaving Packy's, Arlene let out a cry. "I forgot to tell you. The doctor told me that someone called to confirm Charlotte's appointment a few days prior to that. The doctor thought it was me. But it wasn't."

"Meredith? It makes sense. She'd been watching your house. She must have known which road Charlotte always took. If she was the one who'd called to confirm the doctor's appointment, then she would have known when Charlotte would be on the road that day."

"If only Charlotte would have let me drive her to the doctor that day," Arlene said after she joined him in his vehicle, "this wouldn't have happened."

"I wouldn't bet on that. I doubt anything would have stopped Meredith."

"We can go to the sheriff," Arlene said. "We have proof Meredith was in town."

Hank shook his head. "We have a witness who *might* have seen Meredith. Even if we could prove Meredith Foster was in Whitehorse, it doesn't prove she took Charlotte."

"It makes no sense," Arlene said. "Why would Meredith Foster want Charlotte's baby?"

He shook his head. He definitely didn't want to speculate. But if Meredith Foster believed Charlotte was carrying her husband's baby, she might not want another baby out there who had any claim to her husband's attention or his money.

Arlene had paled. She shook her head, tears welling in her brown eyes. "She'll hurt the baby. Hurt it and Charlotte, won't she?"

"No," he said quickly. "If she was going to do that, she would have done it right away. She had Charlotte call you and send the note. She needs Charlotte."

Hank knew his argument had holes in it. But he also knew that he had to give Arlene some hope. "Right now we just have to focus on what we know."

"But if Lucas is the father of Charlotte's baby…" Her voice broke. "Charlotte's lie she was spreading about the older man from out of town being the father got back to Meredith Foster. Don't you see? We have to let Meredith know that the baby is Lucas's. Then she will let Charlotte go."

He wished it were that simple.

Arlene seemed to realize what she was saying. "She can't let Charlotte go, can she? Charlotte can identify her."

"Don't worry. I have a plan." One he hoped to hell would work. He would have to sell Meredith Foster on the idea that a pregnant woman high on hormones could get off easier for kidnapping her husband's supposed pregnant mistress than for a double murder.

He just prayed it wasn't too late.

MEREDITH FOSTER was in her private bedroom, getting dressed to go out, when the call came in. She'd moved into the spare room at her doctor's insistence. At least that's the story she'd told John. He had appeared relieved when she'd told him. Apparently he didn't want to be around her any more than she did him.

But she knew he would do anything for the baby. *His* baby.

"The doctor says I need bed rest and no stress if I hope to carry this baby to term," Meredith had said. "She suggested separate bedrooms until the baby is born."

"Whatever you need, Mer," he'd said.

She hated being called Mer, but she'd bitten her tongue. It was hard not to show how angry she was with him. All of this was his fault. But she suspected he knew that. Just as he knew she would make him pay the rest of his life for it. And once they had their baby, he could damn well take care of it.

She picked up the phone after the third ring, already irritated. John was downstairs, but he wouldn't remember that Delores had been called away on a family emergency so there was no one to cook or clean or do the things they'd been accustomed to her doing for them. Including answering the phone. "Hello?"

"Mrs. Foster. We met the other day at your house. My partner and I were investigating the disappearance of a young pregnant woman? Charlotte Evans?"

"Yes, I recall, although I don't believe I got your name or your partner's."

"I just wanted to apologize."

That surprised her enough that it derailed her before she could insist he answer her question. "Apologize?"

"Yes. We had suspected that the baby Charlotte Evans

was carrying might have been your husband's. That was when we believed she was eight months pregnant. We have since come across evidence that Ms. Evans was pregnant *before* she met your husband—by an old boyfriend. In fact, she is *nine* months pregnant."

Meredith slumped down on the edge of the bed, trying to take all this in as quickly as possible. "So," she said slowly, "you're telling me that my husband has been cleared, is that right?"

"Yes. So I apologize for upsetting either of you. The problem we've run across is Ms. Evans's lack of credibility because of all the lies she's told. Apparently her only intimate contact was with the boyfriend."

Meredith felt her head swim.

"It's been difficult because of her past with the law and, like I said, all the lies. At this point it's a wonder anyone believes anything she says. Also, her mother has had word from her. Now if she just finds her way to a hospital so she can have this baby, we can close our investigation for good. Again my apologies." He hung up.

Meredith sat holding the receiver. She could not believe this. The stupid girl had *lied?* Meredith wanted to scream. All of this had been for nothing. And now there was no getting out of having a baby she didn't want—and all because of some lying little whore?

She threw the phone against the wall. It shattered, plastic flying in every direction.

"Meredith?" John's concerned voice outside in the hall.

She knew she had to gain control of herself. She couldn't let him see her like this. Especially since she feared what she would do to him.

"It's all right, dear. Just one of those telemarketers who wouldn't take no for an answer." She heard him try her door to find it locked. Swearing under her breath, she went to the door and opened it. "I didn't realize I'd locked the door."

He was looking past her to the phone debris on the floor, no doubt wondering why it was necessary for her to lock her door. Especially since this was the first time he'd ever tried to come into her room.

"It's the hormones," she said quickly. "My temper is worse than usual. I really am terrible company tonight. Would you mind giving my apologies to our hostess? I'm not up to going to anyone's house for dinner."

"Of course. Are you sure I shouldn't stay home with you? I don't like the idea of you being here alone in your condition."

Yes, her condition. She might have been touched by his concern if it had been for her—or if she didn't hate the bastard so much at this moment.

"That's sweet," she said. "But I insist. I'm just going to bed early. You go. And tomorrow you can tell me what everyone was wearing."

He frowned. Sometimes the man was so dense.

"I'm joking, John. But I will want a report on her caterer. I'm hoping to use that caterer for our next party. Promise me you will try everything she serves at dinner, including the desserts." That should keep him there long enough anyway.

He stepped back, albeit reluctantly, as she closed the door. She didn't lock it until she heard him drive away. Then she hurriedly changed her clothes. She didn't have much time.

ARLENE WAS AMAZED by how quickly everything fell together the moment they reached Billings. A rented utility van was waiting for them, complete with service uniforms in their sizes, tools, mobile radios and clipboards.

She looked over at Hank. "How did you do all this?"

He smiled. "Let's just say I have a few connections left."

From down the street Hank had called Meredith on a secure cell phone and sewn the seed.

"That's all we can do for now," he'd said after he hung up.

"What if Charlotte is exactly where she said she was—with some man, safe?" Arlene asked. "All of this would be for nothing. Maybe worse. Won't you get in trouble if anyone finds out what you're doing, since you're no longer with the government?"

"Let me worry about that," he said. Just then someone inside the Foster home picked up the phone and began to dial. The number showed up on a readout on the equipment in the back of the van, along with a name. Cara Williamson.

A moment later, a woman answered. "Hello?"

"Cara, it's Meredith. I was hoping we could have lunch tomorrow. I'm going crazy waiting for this baby to come."

"Tomorrow? Let me check. What time were you thinking?"

"Eleven-thirtyish, to avoid the rush. I'm craving that incredible salad they make at Audrey's. Do you mind meeting downtown? I have some errands to run after. Delores, my live-in, had a family emergency, so I'm left high and dry."

"Is everything all right with the baby? I heard the doctor prescribed bed rest."

"For the first few months, but I'm doing so well she's

letting me out, thinks I need the fresh air and exercise," Meredith said. "But these cravings…" Both women laughed, discussed the weather and finally got off the line, promising to see each other the next day at 11:30 a.m. at Audrey's.

"You had their phone tapped?" Arlene said, sounding shocked as the van fell silent. She raised a brow. "Is that…legal?"

He smiled at her. "Yes. If you don't get caught. Don't worry. I have immunity for life."

She raised a brow, not sure she believed that. He just didn't want her worrying about him. She had enough to worry about, he knew. "What now?"

"Now we wait."

It didn't take long. The garage door opened. John Foster backed out in his black sports car. He appeared to be dressed for an engagement.

As he drove off, Arlene said, "He's going without his wife?"

"Unless she's taking her own car."

"What if we're wrong?" she asked when Meredith didn't appear. "What if she doesn't have Charlotte?"

The garage door opened again. Two seconds later, a pregnant Meredith Foster drove out in her silver SUV.

Arlene swore. "That's the same color and type of vehicle that I saw driving by my house. We're going to follow her, aren't we?"

Hank started the van, but before he could shift into gear, another car came out of the darkness of a side street.

He let out a curse as John Foster's black sports car began to tail his wife's SUV.

"The son of a bitch is going to blow the whole thing,"

Hank said as he shifted into gear and joined the parade, staying back a good distance.

They hadn't gone far when he said, "I knew it. She spotted her husband following her. Didn't the dumb SOB realize she would be looking for a tail?"

"Obviously not," Arlene said. "If we're right, he must not know anything."

"But he suspects something if he's tailing her."

Meredith turned into a convenience store. Her husband parked on the street. Hank drove past to circle a block and come back to park far enough away they could watch but not be noticed.

Meredith came out of the convenience store with an ice cream cone and got into her car.

"She doesn't act like she sees him," Arlene said. "Maybe—"

"No, she saw him," Hank said. Meredith turned back the way she'd come. "She's going home. We're not going anywhere tonight."

HANK HAD WANTED to drop Arlene off at a motel, but she wouldn't hear of it.

"I'm staying with you."

"It's not going to be that comfortable in the van all night." He didn't expect Meredith to leave the house again tonight. But he couldn't take the chance she'd leave when her husband, home from wherever he'd gone dressed up like that, was sound asleep.

Hank had known this would put pressure on Meredith. That is, if she had Charlotte. They couldn't be sure of that, and it scared him that while they were killing time in this van Charlotte could be having her baby while being held prisoner by someone else. Someone they couldn't even imagine.

On the way back to the Foster house he'd stopped at a pizza joint, filled up two thermoses with black coffee and bought three large pizzas, loaded.

"Dinner, midnight snack and breakfast," he'd said at Arlene's raised eyebrow.

Every few hours he moved the van. Residents in fancy neighborhoods tended to notice a van parked too long in one spot. Even a utility van. They ate, drank coffee and talked. The van was set up with a monitor, the surveillance camera mounted on the top so they could watch the house from the back and not be seen.

A little after midnight he got a call. He'd set his home phone to forward any calls he got—just in case he heard more on the case.

What he hadn't anticipated was a call from Cameron.

"She's flown."

"What?" he demanded, sitting straight up. "How the hell—"

"Probably the same way she fooled you," Cameron snapped. "I wanted you to know. Just in case."

"Just in case she shows up here?" he demanded.

"Sorry."

Hank swore as he snapped the phone shut. His suspicious mind couldn't help but consider that Rena had been allowed to escape—after she'd been told he was the one who'd identified her from some photographs. They wanted her to come for him. Maybe they hoped he and Rena would kill each other and clean up the mess that way.

Who the hell knew what they wanted? Or if his suspicions weren't just paranoia. It came with the territory.

"What is it?" Arlene asked.

He looked over at her. "It's my old life, the one I tried to protect you from." No chance of that now. He was too deep in Arlene's life to back out now, and she his.

He pulled her to him. Curled up together in front of the monitor, a curtain drawn behind the seats, he told her about Rena. Arlene had to know exactly what the stakes were.

"So what I'm saying is that it could dangerous," he finished. Rena hadn't been the kind of woman who would use someone else to get to him. But then, Rena had gone to the other side, hadn't she?

In the glow of the monitor he saw the look on Arlene's face when he described Rena. "I want you to know what she looks like in case you ever see her, so you can give her a wide berth—and me, as well, should she turn up."

"She sounds like she is a beautiful young woman."

He laughed at that. "In her case, beauty is definitely only skin deep."

Then he told her about himself. He was sick of secrets and he didn't want any between them. But also he wanted her to know who he'd been, *what* he'd been, because he knew they couldn't escape their pasts. He wanted her to know him. Know him in a way Bitsy never had.

"You killed people." Arlene said it so simply, without judgment, without reproach, when he'd finished.

"For my country," he said, his tone laced with sarcasm.

"It haunts you."

"Oh, yeah."

She snuggled against him, her head on his chest. "You and I have that in common, don't we? We both wish we could rewrite the past."

He stroked a hand down her slim back. "I guess we're just going to have to make the best of every minute. Have you ever made love in the back of a van?"

She shook her head as his hand slid inside her shirt to cup her breast.

"Then you definitely haven't lived."

Just before daylight, Arlene dozed.

It wasn't until a little after seven in the morning that the garage door on the Foster house finally purred open once more.

Chapter Ten

Violet Evans had done everything they had asked. She'd being working at one of the nurses' stations as required by the doctors, hating every minute of the horrible graveyard schedule they'd given her and the mind-numbing monotony of the work.

Every day it was harder to pretend to be one of the sane ones. It had been easier to pretend to be crazy. How crazy was that?

She had too much time to think about her life. To remember things she'd forgotten, things that began to haunt her. She'd been a disappointment to her mother, but sometimes when she thought about it, she didn't hear her mother's voice—which surprised her.

It was her grandmother she heard belittling her. *You'll never get that girl married off, Arlene. You'd better teach her to cook. It's the only hope she has of ever getting a man.*

Her grandmother's irritating voice seemed to follow her through her daily duties. At night, Violet would take one of the pills the doctor had prescribed for her after she'd complained of headaches, and that quieted her grandmother for a while.

But lately the voice had been getting more insistent. Violet had been forced to steal extra pills just so she could get some peace.

That girl is a malingerer, Arlene. You going to let her get away with that?

"*Shut up!*" Violet screamed.

"Violet?"

She looked up and realized she was still at the nurses' station, and now the nursing supervisor was watching her closely, looking worried.

"Sorry," she said meekly. "I was talking to myself. It's a song that I got in my head this morning and can't get out," she added, smiling sheepishly. "It's driving me crazy." She realized what she'd said. "You know what I mean."

The nurse nodded, but Violet knew the woman would be keeping a closer eye on her. That's all they did around here—watch you. It was as if they *expected* abnormal behavior, waited for it. Who wouldn't go crazy here?

And she still didn't have a release date. She felt as if it had all been a trick, as though they were pushing her to the edge, seeing if she would break so they could keep her here.

The irony was that she'd put herself in here. She'd used her intelligence to fool the law and the doctors into believing she'd had a breakdown. It had kept her out of prison. She'd pretended to be crazy. And now she was pretending to be sane. No wonder she felt...confused.

That girl is crazy, Arlene. Certifiable. Remember that wagon with the dead cats?

Violet shook her head frantically. *I didn't do anything to the cats. It wasn't me. I didn't do it. Noooooooo.* She looked up, hoping she'd only thought the word—not spoken again.

"I think you've worked enough for one day," the nurse said.

"No, I'm fine. I need to finish filing these." Violet stared down at the papers in her hand. Is that what she'd been doing? Filing? She couldn't remember.

The nurse gently took the papers from her. "You're overwrought. Why don't you lie down for a while?"

Violet nodded and stepped out from the behind the desk. She stopped in the middle of hall, and for a moment she couldn't remember where her room was. Stress. It short-fused her brain. That and all the drugs they'd given her.

Well, at least now we know what happened to those cats that kept disappearing, don't we?

"Violet?" the nurse asked behind her. "Are you sure you're all right?"

"Tired," she said, realizing that she'd put her hands over her ears to shut out the sound of her grandmother's voice. How crazy was that, since her grandmother was dead? "I didn't realize I was so tired."

She heard a bell ding behind her and an instant later a young orderly was at her elbow.

"Show Violet to her room," said the nurse. "Make sure she takes her medication."

Violet felt a hand on her elbow and then she was moving down the hall in a direction she would have sworn she'd never been before.

Do you need any more proof that something is wrong with that girl, Arlene? A wagon full of dead cats. It's enough to scare the wits out of you. You can't let this get out. Imagine what people would say about this family if they knew. And we all know who they'd blame, don't we, Arlene?

"I didn't do anything to the cats," Violet whimpered as the orderly led her down the hall. "I found them like that. I thought I could…" But she couldn't remember what she'd planned to do with them.

As she crawled up onto her bed into a fetal position, she saw herself at her bedroom window watching her mother in the yard below with an eerie kind of fascination. Her mother had been crying. Violet could tell by the way Arlene's body seemed to jerk with sobs. She'd never seen her mother cry before, especially like that.

It had been strange watching her usually stoic mother digging a hole and dropping the dead cats into it, her body convulsing with sobs, face stained with tears, her strangled words barely audible through the open window, "Violet, oh, my baby girl, what have you done?"

ARLENE WOKE TO daylight and Hank still watching the monitor. The street was quiet, as was the Foster house, but the sun was up. She could feel the glow of it coming through the curtains and wondered, as she did every morning, where Charlotte was and if she was all right.

A part of her still believed that Charlotte had taken off with some man. Just as Hank had told Meredith, the girl lied so much that it was hard to believe she hadn't told yet another man that he was the father of her baby—and probably had, if the mood struck her.

"Good morning," Hank said more cheerfully than she would have had she stayed up all night.

"Good morning." She sat up, knowing he'd seen the worry on her face and was doing his best to relieve her mind. She thought of his confession last night and knew how hard that had been for him. As hard as her telling him about her children and the terrible job she felt she'd done with them.

"Cold pizza," he offered.

She shook her head. "I'm fine."

He reached out and stroked her cheek. "You look beautiful in the morning."

"I can well imagine," she said with a laugh.

Suddenly his gaze darted to the monitor, and she instantly sobered as she watched the garage door yawn open.

"Let's get dressed," he said as John Foster drove out in his black sports car and the garage door slid shut.

"What about Meredith?" she asked as she quickly shed what little clothing she was wearing to put on the utility workman uniform, complete with cap.

"If we have to, we'll trick her out of the house, but I'm willing to bet she doesn't spend a lot of time cleaning the place," Hank said. "Even pregnant, I'd bet she has a very active social life. Also, if she has Charlotte, then she will know she's being watched. After last night, she knows that even her husband is watching her, so she'll stick rigidly to her normal schedule."

JOHN FOSTER FOUGHT panic as he drove to work. Those FBI agents, even working in an unofficial capacity, asking questions about the girl, had him more than rattled. Add to that the strange way Meredith had been acting. He'd tried to write it off as her just being pregnant, hormones, as she'd said.

But he was worried. If Meredith had known about the girl, what would she have done?

He felt sick and scared, and it was all he could do not to get on the interstate and make a run for it.

We couldn't be happier, could we, John? Meredith's voice echoed in his head from the night she'd announced she was pregnant.

He couldn't leave his child. Wasn't that exactly the reason Meredith had gotten pregnant?

She'd never wanted children. She'd made that perfectly clear. At one point she'd even demanded he have a vasectomy. It was one of the few times he'd stood his ground. Had he known then that he would try to leave her one day? That he might want a chance for happiness with another woman?

He and Meredith hadn't been intimate for months after that. Hell, they hardly were now. He was surprised she'd managed to get pregnant.

Except she'd been more loving after he'd returned from Whitehorse, he thought now. Oh, God, had she known even then?

If not, she'd suspected. He'd been such a fool. Her getting pregnant, and the girl, Charlotte Evans, getting pregnant with his child, as well. He wasn't stupid enough to think it was a coincidence, not knowing Meredith the way he did. She knew about Charlotte. And now she had him trapped.

Not that he hadn't felt trapped all his life. His family

and Meredith's had been friends from before the time the two were born. Just a year apart, the families had always joked that John and Meredith would marry.

Unfortunately his father and Meredith's were also in business together, and it became quite clear to John that he was expected to marry Meredith. He'd made the mistake of dating her a few times to appease his parents. Meredith had given herself to him and he'd taken her up on it. Hell, sex was sex. But then two months later she'd called him to tell him she was pregnant.

John had felt he had no choice, had never had a choice, not about going to work for his father or about marrying Meredith. It wasn't until after the huge, expensive wedding when they were on their way to St. Thomas for their honeymoon, that Meredith told him she'd lost the baby.

He'd suspected she'd never been pregnant. He had tried to make the best of it. Meredith had made it clear early on that they were married for life. John knew what he would lose if he left Meredith: his job, his family, everything he'd worked for. He'd be lucky to get out with his life.

After ten years of marriage, he'd gotten to the point that he couldn't take it anymore. Willing to give up everything to be free, he'd asked Meredith for a divorce. He'd left the house not caring what happened.

He'd gotten into his car and headed north, not having any idea where he would go or what he would do. The freedom was intoxicating. He found himself in the small western town of Whitehorse, Montana. He'd rented a motel room and gone out to dinner. A young blond woman had waited on him. She didn't even look of legal age.

John had gone back a second time. He felt sorry for the

girl. She'd dropped some dishes. He'd given her a large tip. She'd been grateful and had asked him to wait for her, since she was getting off for the night, something about needing a ride home.

That was the last thing he remembered except for nightmarish bits of memory until he woke up in a strange motel room with the reek of the young blonde's perfume all over him and the girl in bed beside him.

He'd never been unfaithful to Meredith. That morning with the girl in his bed, he could just see the headlines when he was arrested for sleeping with an underage girl. He'd hightailed it out of Whitehorse, running back to Meredith. A mistake, of course, in hindsight.

He'd never dreamed he might have gotten the girl pregnant. Or that Meredith would find out and trick him into getting her pregnant, as well.

And now the girl was missing and the FBI was involved. They knew what he'd done, believed him to be the father of the baby, probably thought he'd done something with the girl.

John Foster couldn't imagine things getting any worse.

Unless, of course, Meredith had done something to that poor pregnant girl.

HANK WATCHED THE monitor and waited. He'd been a little jumpy ever since he'd heard that Rena was on the loose again, but he'd tried to hide it from Arlene.

What had worried him as he'd stayed awake last night on the surveillance was why *hadn't* Rena settled the old score with him?

It had been almost a year. How many kills had she done

in that amount of time? Or was the one in Prague the first? Where had she been all this time?

In a hospital recuperating? Strange how that thought pricked him to his soul. Doing away with enemies of the state was one thing. Wounding one of them was another.

What a screwed-up job he'd had. No wonder Bitsy hadn't been able to take it. He'd never told her exactly what he did. Had she suspected? All Bitsy had known was that he'd worked with a female operative for a while. Until Rena had defected to the other side. Until she'd become enemy number one.

"Are you all right?" Arlene asked.

He glanced over at her and nodded. It hadn't just been Rena who'd kept him up last night. He was worried about Arlene because he feared that they might already be too late to save Charlotte and the baby.

Worse, he feared that if Meredith Foster had abducted Charlotte, it was because of the lie Charlotte had told about John Foster. A lie that could have already cost Charlotte her life. And all because Charlotte apparently didn't want anyone knowing that Lucas Bronson was the father of her baby.

Oh, the tangled web we weave, he thought.

He'd considered taking what circumstantial evidence they had to the sheriff. Better yet, the FBI. But he knew that with Charlotte's phone call and the note, coupled with her past behavior with the law, they wouldn't get more than lip service.

Also, Hank knew how the FBI worked. The agents wouldn't have been doing any more than he was doing right now. Actually, a lot less, he thought, since the phone tap would have been illegal without a warrant and they couldn't have gotten a warrant with such flimsy evidence.

The garage door opened again and he breathed a sigh of relief. He could feel the clock ticking and hoped to hell he was doing the right thing by not turning this over to someone who wasn't involved with the mother of the alleged missing girl. Would Arlene forgive him if he made the wrong move and Charlotte and the baby suffered for it?

As the back of the SUV swung up, Meredith Foster appeared with a dry-cleaning bag and several department store shopping sacks, as if returning items. She was dressed up for her luncheon engagement with her friend Cara.

She slammed the trunk door, looking very pregnant, and disappeared back into the garage. A moment later, the silver SUV backed out and sped off down the street toward downtown Billings, making him wonder if he wasn't chasing the wrong suspect.

Hank called the home phone just to make sure that Delores was gone as Meredith had said. The live-in's car wasn't on the street where it had been last time. He'd seen it and run the plates.

The phone rang and rang and finally the answering machine picked up.

He hung up without leaving a message and looked over at Arlene. "Ready?"

THE FOSTER HOUSE had a security system, state-of-the-art, the kind Hank had been trained in years ago.

Within minutes he and Arlene, dressed in their utility company uniforms, with him carrying a toolbox, headed for the back door.

Within seconds they were in the house, the system disarmed. He handed Arlene a pair of latex gloves. "Put these on. Leave everything just as it was. You start upstairs." He handed her a small two-way radio. "I'll signal you if we need to get out quickly."

She nodded, clipped the radio to her belt as he had done and snapped on the gloves, her face set in determination.

"Ten minutes. See what you can find," he said, knowing he didn't have to explain to her what they were looking for.

He took the office. The entire place was too neat and clean. It felt like one of those model homes where no one lives. Even Arlene's, with the plastic covers on the couch and chairs, was more inviting.

The office, which he found at once, contained little. One three-drawer cherry file cabinet that matched the desk and chair. The top desk drawer had the usual: pens, extra box of staples, thumbtacks, paper clips, white-out and stamps. The two other drawers contained envelopes, paper and bills to be paid.

Hank sorted through the mail twice seeing nothing except the usual household bills. No rental records for some hideaway to keep a young pregnant girl. He hadn't expected Meredith Foster to be that foolish. She hadn't been.

The file cabinet was locked. He found the key under the box of staples in the top desk drawer.

Like the rest of the office, the file cabinet offered nothing of interest except insight into the Fosters. Both seemed to be meticulous to the extreme.

If either of them had something to do with Charlotte

being missing, then the abduction would have been well planned.

Something was bothering him. He couldn't put his finger on it until he had searched the rest of the downstairs.

He backtracked to the office. Medical bills. John Foster had said his wife was having a difficult pregnancy. Meredith had indicated the same thing. But he couldn't remember seeing any in the mail.

He opened the file cabinet again and pulled out the file marked *Medical* and riffled through the papers.

Dr. Florence Springer. Hank memorized the name and address. He knew why he hadn't picked up on it earlier. There were only a couple of paid bills from Dr. Springer in the file.

Maybe Meredith had been seeing a specialist. But then, where were the invoices?

In the back of the file cabinet was a box marked *Canceled Checks.*

One quick peek was all he needed. All of the checks were signed in Meredith Foster's no-nonsense neat hand.

Of course Meredith would do the bills. No checks to another doctor.

As he closed the file cabinet, locked it, replacing the key in the drawer, he heard Arlene come into the room and looked up. One look, and he knew she'd found something.

ARLENE CLUTCHED the book in her hands to keep from shaking.

"What did you find?" Hank asked.

"This was next to her bed, on the bookshelf with some other books about babies and pregnancy."

"Nothing unusual about that, since she's pregnant," Hank said.

"Except this one was wedged behind the others." She handed him the book, her hand trembling from the shock of what she'd found. "Check out the pages she has marked."

He glanced at the title of the book, then let the pages fall open to the receipt Meredith Foster had been using as a bookmark.

Hank closed the book after a moment to study the title. She watched him school his expression.

"C-sections aren't that unusual, especially in high-risk pregnancies," he said. "She'd read up on them."

"It's a *medical* book." Her voice broke. "Why would she need to know how to perform the surgery?"

"Put the book back exactly as you found it," he said, glancing at his watch. "We have to get out now."

"Hank—"

"We can talk in the van. I'll meet you in the kitchen."

She'd hoped he would relieve her growing fear about Charlotte and the baby. He'd tried, but she knew that the medical book and the marked page had upset him as much as it had her. Only he was better at hiding his reaction.

She hurried up the stairs to the spare bedroom where it was clear that Meredith had been staying and did as he'd instructed, trying not to let her fear get the best of her. Now more than ever she couldn't fall apart.

She was waiting in the kitchen, standing on the expensive Italian tile, not touching anything, making herself as small as possible, when he suddenly appeared.

She'd never known anyone who could move so quietly. He motioned toward the back door they'd come in. She followed. Once outside, she took a gasping breath. The air was hot and close and she felt as if she were suffocating.

He reset the alarm, stripped off his gloves. She did the same, stuffing them into her pocket just as he had done. Then he took her arm as he led her along the side of the house until they were almost to the spot where the elaborate landscaping that blocked any view of the neighbors ended.

He stopped to pick up the toolbox from where he'd ditched it. Arlene made sure her hair was tucked under her cap. He gave her a thumbs-up and, with toolbox in hand, walked casually to the service van parked at the curb.

It wasn't until they were inside the van and several blocks away that she finally felt she could breathe. She fought the fear that threatened to overwhelm her. She could feel the clock ticking. Charlotte could have the baby at any moment. Maybe already had.

Was she alone? Scared?

Arlene fought back the tears that closed her throat. What if something horrible had happened to Charlotte and the baby, and that it was too late? *They* were too late?

Hank parked the van. She felt his hand on her arm. She turned to him.

"I know you're scared. But, believe me, I'm trying to find her as fast as possible."

She nodded. "I know. Thank you. Meredith did something with Charlotte and the baby, didn't she?"

"I think it's possible given what we know now. Let me see what I can find out, all right? Will you be okay out here for a few minutes?"

"Don't worry about me. Just do whatever it is you do,"

she said, just then realizing that he'd parked in front of a cell phone company.

"I'll be right back."

She watched him go, wondering what she would have done without him. Certainly not have broken into anyone's home. Or even tracked down John Foster. And she knew how far she would have gotten with law enforcement.

As she waited, she did something she'd never done. She prayed.

HANK BOUGHT A CELL phone and some minutes, then dialed numbers he'd told himself he'd forgotten.

"Need some medical information on one Meredith Foster. Doctor's name is Florence Springer." He gave the name of Meredith's insurance company, complete with address. "Looking for pregnancy information. Need it ASAP. Will hold."

He stood in the shade of the building, watching his SUV. He could just make out Arlene inside. When he'd seen the medical book, the chapter on C-sections falling open too easily where it had been marked, he'd tried not to let her see his concern.

But Arlene was sharp. She knew. She'd known when she found the book.

"Information ready to transmit," the voice on the other end of the line acknowledged. "Protected e-mail address?"

He rattled off a secure e-mail address. What would they do without computers? "How soon should I have that?"

"Sending it now."

He hung up and walked back to his vehicle and Arlene. Reaching behind his seat, he picked up the laptop computer and turned it on. The van came stocked with wireless Internet. Once on the Internet, he checked the special account he'd set up.

There it was. Quickly he scanned through Meredith Foster's confidential medical records, once, twice—and let out an expletive as he looked up at Arlene.

"Tell me," she said and seemed to brace herself.

"Meredith Foster *isn't* pregnant."

Chapter Eleven

They watched the Foster house from a distance via the monitor in the back of the van. Hank had gotten them more food before returning to the house. He'd checked to make sure no one had been there since they'd left earlier.

No one had.

It was almost six in the evening by the time John Foster's little black car pulled into the drive.

Meredith hadn't returned, and Hank had felt his worry escalate with each passing hour.

"Doesn't look as if John will be getting a hot meal tonight," Arlene said. "You don't think she—"

"We're about to find out," Hank said as he started the engine and drove down to the Foster house.

John Foster was just getting out of his car and hadn't even had time to close the garage door. He looked up as the van roared up.

The man stood like a deer caught in the headlights as Hank and Arlene got out and walked toward him. They still wore their utility service uniforms, but Arlene saw that John recognized them.

"I thought I answered all your questions," he said, already sounding panicked. If he wondered why they were dressed as they were, he didn't ask.

"Where is your wife?" Hank demanded.

"My wife? She's gone to visit a friend. You upset her. She's pregnant and could lose the baby." He sounded distraught.

"Let's step inside," Hank said calmly.

John Foster fumbled his cell phone out. "I think I'm going to call the police. This is harassment."

"Your wife isn't pregnant," Hank snapped. "She never was. She faked the whole thing. And, unless I miss my guess, she abducted Charlotte Evans and intends to take her baby—one way or the other." He stopped. "I thought you were going to call the police?"

John Foster had frozen in motion, the cell phone in his hand. Suddenly he dropped the phone. It hit the concrete garage floor and bounced.

Hank caught it before it could bounce again and handed it back. "We need to find your wife before she does something we're all going to regret. Now, shall we step inside?"

John nodded and turned to lead them into the house. Hank closed the garage door behind them and followed.

"Where did she say she was going?" Hank asked as soon as they were standing in the kitchen.

"She didn't say. She was angry with me and said she needed time alone to think. She knows about me and Charlotte."

Hank swore. "I called Meredith last night and told her it wasn't your baby. You never slept with Charlotte. She drugged you and only planned to tell you that you'd impregnated her. Apparently she'd planned to have you help with expenses. She never got around to doing that, right?"

His eyes widened. "No. Meredith knew last *night?*"

"I guess she didn't tell you," Hank said.

John Foster pulled out a chair at the breakfast nook and dropped into it.

"I'll make coffee," Arlene said and Hank nodded his approval.

John looked stunned as he dropped his head in his hands.

"Where would she go?"

"I don't know."

"She has a cell phone with her, right?"

He nodded.

"What's the number?" As John gave it to him, Hank scribbled down the number into a small notebook.

Arlene watched for a moment, then asked, "Where do you keep the coffee?"

John shook his head. He looked dazed. "I don't know."

Hank heard Arlene going through the cupboards. She found the coffee and got a pot going, the smell filling the kitchen as he continued to question John Foster.

"Does her cell phone have GPS on it?" Hank asked.

John shrugged. "I suppose so. She always likes the best that money can buy." He looked alarmed that he'd said that. "Not that she doesn't deserve it."

"Your wife *lied* to you."

"I just can't believe Meredith would do anything like this."

"Can't you?" Hank asked.

John Foster took the cup of hot coffee Arlene offered

him, clutching it in both hands like a life raft. He took a sip, then another, and seemed to grow a little stronger.

"Look," Hank said. "Meredith has to be checking on Charlotte, so wherever the girl is being held must be close. Do you have a summer cabin, a condo, a favorite place you go? A friend who she might have watching Charlotte?"

His head came up slowly. He blinked. "She has a friend who owns a place in Red Lodge. It's about thirty miles south of here in the mountains."

Hank shot Arlene a look. "Is there a phone up there?"

John shook his head. "No cell phone service either."

"Can you draw us a map how to get there?"

John nodded as Hank handed him the notebook and pen.

Hank swore. He'd watched Meredith load a lot of things into the SUV—from the rear. She'd wanted them to see her. She'd known they would be watching. Just as she had to have known her phone was tapped. That's why she'd made the luncheon appointment on her land line. She'd probably canceled it via her cell phone later.

He'd been had. He should have followed her. But if he hadn't gotten into the house, he wouldn't have known she wasn't pregnant. Not that that information didn't seem pretty worthless right now.

It wouldn't help find Charlotte. But at least he had a pretty good idea of why Meredith had taken Charlotte. She wanted the baby. Apparently planned to try to pass it off as her own.

What had she planned to do with Charlotte, though? That worried him. That and the fact that Meredith knew they were onto her. How did that change things?

Would she make a run for it? Or did she think she could

still get away with this? There was no evidence against Meredith at this point. If Charlotte was never found…

He didn't want to go down that road. He had to find her—and fast.

As meticulous as Meredith was, she'd planned ahead, probably taking a suitcase to wherever she had Charlotte stashed—maybe even before she'd abducted the girl. She probably had the rest figured out, as well, a story about her baby being born earlier, away from a hospital, then showing up with Charlotte's baby. No one would have been the wiser, since apparently she'd had John fooled from day one.

Meredith could have gotten away with it.

"We're going to need a photograph of your wife," he told John as he tore the map from the notebook and handed it to Arlene. While John went to get a photo, Hank asked Arlene, "How you holding up?"

"Okay," she said.

He smiled at her, dropping a hand to her shoulder to rub her neck for a moment. He could tell she was on edge but trying hard to remain strong. He'd never met a more courageous woman. If this had been his daughter, his grandchild…

John returned with the photo and Hank asked Arlene to wait for him in the van. Then he turned to Foster.

"If you hear from your wife, you call me immediately. Do not tell her that we were here or that you know she isn't pregnant. If you do that, she will have no reason to keep Charlotte Evans or her baby alive. Do you understand?"

John shuddered. "Meredith wouldn't—"

"Your wife is in a very delicate mental state right now. One little push…"

"I understand."

"Good. Give me your cell phone number. I want to be able to reach you."

Foster seemed more together as he gave him the number, but still Hank worried.

"If you hear anything from her, you'll call me, right? You still have my number?"

John Foster nodded. "What will happen to Meredith if all this is true?"

"If will depend on if we can stop her in time."

ARLENE TRIED NOT to think. But it was impossible. She could imagine Charlotte, pregnant and afraid, being held prisoner by some stranger. Her baby girl. Charlotte had never been strong. She was the sensitive one, the one who seemed the most affected by any problems in the family.

With an awful feeling in the pit of her stomach, Arlene thought about how Charlotte had taken up for her sister Violet, taking that pain out on drunks at the bar. She shivered. What would Charlotte do under these circumstances? Unable to defend even herself, let alone her baby.

If Hank hadn't persisted… Arlene hated to think how badly she'd wanted to believe the phone call from Charlotte, the note. She hadn't wanted to face that anything could have happened to her daughter. That some crazy woman had abducted her and—

She brushed at the tears that burned her eyes as she watched Hank hurry toward the van. She couldn't panic. She'd been holding it together. That's what she'd always done. She was the strong one. She was the one who had always protected her family as best she could.

And now she had Hank on her side.

Meredith didn't know that they knew she wasn't pregnant. She wouldn't hurt the baby. If Charlotte hadn't had the baby yet, if she was being held in this cabin…

They would find her. Get there in time. Charlotte and the baby would be safe. And Meredith Foster would be locked up for a very long time.

She had to believe that.

"What is it?" she asked as Hank climbed behind the wheel of the van and she saw the frown on his face.

"Nothing." He sighed, looked over at her and added, "It's Foster. The guy worries me, that's all."

"Worries you how?" she asked as Hank started the van and they took off south toward Red Lodge.

"His reactions seem all wrong. Maybe it just takes him longer to assimilate what's going on." He gave her a reassuring smile and reached for her hand. "It's probably just me."

Arlene doubted that. Hank had great instincts. From the beginning he'd thought Charlotte's disappearance was suspect.

THE ELEVATION changed more than two thousand feet as they drove from Billings to Red Lodge at the base of Red Lodge Mountain. They drove through the turn-of-the-century downtown, with its sandstone and brick edifices of the late 1800s. Red Lodge was best known as the start of the sixty-eight-mile long Beartooth Highway, a gateway to the high country.

"According to the map, you go out of town toward the

Red Lodge Mountain ski resort for four-point-four miles," Arlene said, reading what John Foster had written.

The day cooled as they reached the dense pines at the foot of the mountain.

"Take the next right."

Hank did, then pulled off the road and into the trees. "I'm going on foot from here." She watched him strap on a holster and check the gun to make sure it was loaded.

"I'm going with you." It must have been her tone.

He glanced over at her, seemed to hesitate, then nodded. "Just stay behind me. And if all hell breaks loose, you dive for the dirt."

Arlene followed him as they kept to the trees. The evening was hot. Only the shade of the pines cooled the still air. According to the map, the cabin was just over the next rise.

Hank stopped, motioned her to silence as he pulled out a pair of small binoculars and crawled up the hill. She followed, doing as he did. When she reached him, he handed her the binoculars. She peered down at a small log cabin. There were no vehicles in sight. But there was a barn not far from the cabin.

She lowered the binoculars and handed them back to Hank.

"We'll check the barn first," he whispered, and she nodded, seeing no other place Meredith could have stashed her silver SUV.

The sky darkened behind the mountains as the sun made its descent and the first breath of cool air moved over them. The fragrant scent of pine grew stronger as they worked their way through the trees to the barn.

The barn was old, probably part of a ranch that had since subdivided. Hank tried the door, keeping his eye on the cabin. Arlene fought the urge to storm up to the cabin. If Charlotte was in there…

The barn door yawned open with a groan. Dust motes danced in the dim light, the smell of hay as strong as that of old manure. No silver SUV.

Hank turned to her and motioned toward the cabin. Arlene was sure that, like her, he suspected they would find the cabin empty, as well.

This wasn't where Meredith had taken Charlotte. Arlene felt the weight of her worry drag at her as they worked their way to the back of the cabin. Hank peered in one of the windows and shook his head.

The cabin was small and open. And empty.

"WHERE'S DELORES?"

Hank looked over at Arlene behind the wheel of his SUV. She'd offered to drive, since he hadn't gotten any sleep last night. He hadn't been able to sleep, though, too keyed up and upset.

He hadn't been paying any attention and now saw that they were almost back to Whitehorse. They hadn't passed another car in miles. The land lay dark beneath the starlit big sky, the headlights carving a narrow swath of gold through the darkness as they sped along the two-lane road. For the last hundred and fifty miles there had been no towns, nothing but open country.

"Delores?" he repeated, tired and discouraged and starting to feel the effects of no sleep.

"I don't think she's been at the house since the first time

we were there," Arlene said. She'd obviously given this some thought. "Didn't you notice the dust?"

"Dust?"

"And when I was looking for coffee, I saw that the refrigerator was almost empty except for some frozen dinners."

It took him a moment to catch up. He was still back on the dust. The Fosters were meticulous. The house spotless. At least the first time he and Arlene had been there.

He sat up, coming fully awake, his brain finally catching up. "Delores."

He snatched up his cell phone. "I need everything you can get me on a woman named Delores. No last name. She is in the employ of John and Meredith Foster of Billings, Montana, and I suspect has been for some time."

"It was just a nightmare," Violet repeated for the third time. She'd come out of the dream to find two orderlies holding her down on the bed and the doctor standing by, looking concerned.

"Perhaps we should try a different medication," the doctor said as he studied Violet now.

She noticed that the orderlies hadn't left the room. What were they expecting her to do?

"I'm fine. Of course I was combative. You would have been, too, if you woke up and two men were holding you down." She just wanted them to leave. "I just need to go back to sleep."

He frowned. "Have you been having trouble sleeping?"

She knew better than to lie. "It's excitement. Isn't it normal that I'm excited about the idea of life outside these walls?" *Escaping this hell hole.*

"I can understand that," he said slowly. "Are you worried you might not be able to cope on the outside?"

She warned herself not to answer too quickly. "Not *worried*. Of course I'm anxious. But I feel, after all the help I've gotten here with you and the other doctors, that I can do it. I want to do it. I want to make you proud."

He beamed and rose from the chair he'd pulled up beside her bed. "Good."

"How much longer do you think it will be?" she couldn't stop herself from asking.

"Well…" He didn't look at her and she knew. That bitch of a nurse had reported her odd behavior, and now this. "I'm thinking a few more weeks couldn't hurt. Let's see how you are then."

It was all she could do not to start screaming again, only this nightmare was real. She was never getting out of here.

She looked down and blinked away tears of fury. He put his hand on her shoulder. He had no idea how much she wanted to grab that hand and break every bone in it.

"Patience. You're doing well at your in-patient job here. That will look good to the board. You've made such miraculous improvements while here that we want to make sure there is no backsliding. You're our prized case."

One irony after another, Violet thought. She'd done such a good acting job that now she was their prized case and they were afraid that she would embarrass them. Just great.

"What's a few more weeks?"

Was the man insane?

She said nothing, couldn't have spoken a word. No, if she had tried, she would have howled, and he would have seen a side of her that would have struck fear to his very core and put those stupid thug orderlies on her again.

Part of her wished she could have let her fury fly, just let it loose on him, just to see the expression on his face.

A few more weeks.

As she lay back down and closed her eyes, Violet knew she couldn't stay here any longer. She'd been paying attention to deliveries, even flirted with one of the older drivers a few times.

She wouldn't be staying a few more weeks. She wouldn't even be staying a few more days.

That girl is a cunning little thing, Arlene, the way she always manages to get her way.

"Yes, Grandmother," Violet whispered and smiled as the doctor and orderlies closed the door behind them. "Aren't I, though?"

Her name is Delores Gonzales formerly of Mexicali, Mexico.

"An illegal?" Hank asked as he paced the floor. He'd been pacing ever since he'd dropped Arlene off at her house and returned home. Time was running out. Once Charlotte had her baby...

"*Was* illegal, but her employer, Meredith Foster, helped her get American citizenship."

Hank let out a low whistle. Delores would be indebted to Meredith in a big way. She would probably do anything her employer asked of her—even keep a pregnant girl prisoner.

He thought about what Meredith had said about Delores having a family emergency.

"Any family in the States?"

"An older sister. She is applying for citizenship through the Fosters, as well, and is also employed by the Fosters. Juanita Gonzales Mendez. Husband Juan deceased."

Hank swore under his breath. "Do you have an address?"

"Both are listed at the Foster residence."

He remembered the red minivan he'd seen parked in front of the Foster house. "What do they drive?"

"Delores Gonzales drives a minivan." He read off the make, model and plate number. It was new and expensive. Meredith either paid her well or provided the ride. "The other doesn't have a license. Nor a car listed in her name."

"Thanks. I owe you."

"Yeah, you do." The man dropped his voice to a whisper. "It hasn't escaped anyone that you've been getting inside assistance. Thought I should warn you."

"Thanks." Hank hung up as he heard the sound of a motorcycle coming up the drive. He walked out to the porch as the rider dismounted and came toward him. "Lucas Bronson, right?"

The young man was tall and lean, clad all in black leather except for the red bandanna tied around his head. No helmet. Kids his age didn't believe they were mortal. Hank remembered that age well. Hell, he still thought he was immortal at times.

Lucas stopped at the bottom of the porch steps to narrow his eyes at Hank. "Arlene said you're trying to find Charlotte."

"What do you want to know?" Hank asked.

"I want to know where Charlotte is," Lucas snapped. "I want to help find her." There was a strained passion in the young man's voice that Hank felt.

"Come on in, then," he said and turned and walked back into the house.

Lucas came in like a dog that's been beaten for coming in the house.

"Have a seat," Hank told him. Bitsy used to say he felt more at home with homeless people than with polite society. He smiled at the memory because it was true.

Lucas eyed the leather furniture for a moment.

"Sit. Tea or a soft drink?"

"You got a cola?"

Hank came back with a cold cola from the fridge. Lucas was perched on the edge of one of the leather chairs. Hank handed him the pop and dropped into a chair across from him to keep from pacing.

"So what did you find out about the old guy?" Lucas asked.

Hank smiled, knowing the "old guy" Lucas was referring to was John Foster, who was a good ten years younger than himself. A part of him wanted to challenge the punk kid to an arm-wrestling match just to show him what a really "old guy" could do. But that was such an "old guy" thing to do.

"John Foster?" he asked instead.

Lucas nodded.

Hank filled him in on what they knew. "You have any ideas?"

Lucas shook his head, worry in his expression. "She could be having the baby right now." He met Hank's gaze. "I'm the father. She didn't run around with other guys. She never has. I know she's done some things she shouldn't have, but she's a good kid. I love her and I'm going to marry her."

"That's just it, Lucas—she's a kid. And now that kid is about to have a baby. You're still a kid yourself. How do you plan to support her and yourself, let alone a baby?"

"I've got some ideas."

"Any of them include an education? Maybe an occupation?"

"Yeah, as a matter of fact, Charlotte wants to go to college. She just didn't think Arlene could afford it with her old man splitting like he did."

"Arlene can afford it," Hank said confidently. "But she said Charlotte's never had any interest in going. Charlotte barely finished high school."

"Yeah, well, maybe she's changed. She wants the best for her baby," Lucas said. "That's why she was thinking about giving it up like her mother wanted her to."

"But you plan to talk her out of that," Hank reminded him.

Lucas shrugged and swigged down some of the cola. "I want the best for my kid, too. I don't want him having a family like mine."

"Him?"

"Yeah, didn't Charlotte tell Arlene? The baby's a *boy.*"

AFTER HANK LEFT, Arlene started up the porch steps, but then she heard Bo's stereo and wasn't in the mood to fight with him, so she walked back into the trees behind the house. She could hear the phone if it rang. Floyd had had a bell put in so he could hear the phone when he was working in the barn.

She didn't have to ask Bo to know that he'd made no effort to get a job. Or move out. She'd have to pack his things, leave them on the porch, have the locks on the house changed. How did other parents handle it when their grown children returned home and refused to leave?

She had no idea. All she knew was that she had to put him out. It was the only way he would ever become a responsible adult. Things couldn't keep going the way they were.

It was easier to worry about Bo than Charlotte. Just the thought of her youngest daughter was like a toothache that just kept getting worse until she didn't think she could stand the pain any longer.

Earlier, she'd called Bo on her way home. He'd said there hadn't been any more calls from Charlotte. No more mail either.

She sat down on the old picnic table under the big cottonwoods. She needed to be alone. To think.

It was hard not to panic. If Lucas was right, then Charlotte was nine months pregnant. Her first baby could come late. Maybe there was time.

Or maybe Meredith Foster would get antsy, especially now that she knew they were onto her.

Arlene wouldn't let herself think about what Meredith might do now. Her only hope was that a woman like Meredith was so used to things going her way she wouldn't panic and do anything stupid.

But where did she have Charlotte hidden?

She had abducted a very pregnant woman. She wouldn't have been able to drug her for fear of hurting the baby. So what had she done? Tied her up? Held her at gunpoint?

It was a three-hour drive from Whitehorse to Billings. How could Meredith try to make Charlotte as comfortable as possible—and yet at the same time keep her from getting away?

She pulled out her cell phone and dialed Hank's number. She needed to hear his voice. But she also had a feeling so strong she couldn't ignore it any longer.

"I have a theory," she said the moment he answered. She spelled it out for him.

"I was just getting ready to call you. Delores Gonzales was an illegal. Meredith helped her get her U.S. citizenship. She also helped Delores's older sister, Juanita. I think Meredith has them taking care of Charlotte."

Arlene grasped onto the news, telling herself at least someone was with Charlotte, taking care of her. "Charlotte isn't down by Billings. She's up here somewhere. Maybe close by. I feel it, Hank. Isn't there some way to find out where? You asked about GPS on Meredith's phone...."

"That only works if there is service in that area," he said. "But we tried another way. You know how parents can tell if their kid is where he said he was going to be via computer and the kid's phone? It didn't tell us where Meredith is. But by expanding the area outside of Billings, it did tell us where she isn't."

Arlene felt her throat choke off, her eyes filling with tears. "She's up here, isn't she?"

"It appears that way," Hank said. "Are you sure you wouldn't feel better here with me?"

She wanted nothing more than to be in his arms right now. "No, I need to stay here." In case Charlotte showed up. She knew it was crazy. But if Charlotte managed to get away...

JOHN FOSTER COULDN'T sit still. He'd tried to reach his wife, but she had her cell phone turned off. He'd left messages. She hadn't returned his calls.

He wanted to kill her, feared he would if she came in the door right now. How could she do something like this? Was she crazy?

The periodic unexplained disappearances. Delores leaving so abruptly. Juanita already gone somewhere. Meredith's supposed risky pregnancy. The way she'd moved into the spare bedroom almost at once and kept him at arm's length.

He'd been relieved. He hadn't wanted to have sex with her anyway. But she wasn't even pregnant. Just like the first time.

His wife was a liar and worse.

What if they couldn't catch her before she did something to that poor pregnant girl? Meredith didn't really still believe she could get away with this, did she?

Knowing Meredith, she did. She would come home with a baby. His baby. Except now he knew it wasn't his baby. And she knew it. DNA tests would prove it.

No, even Meredith didn't think she could get away with this now. She would have to cover her tracks. He shuddered at the thought.

The phone rang, making him jump. He stared it as it rang again. Meredith? He recalled what the FBI agent had told him as he started to answer it.

If he told Meredith that he knew she wasn't pregnant, what would she do?

Turn herself in. Return the girl and the baby unharmed. The court would probably be lenient with her. She could be out of prison in a matter of years. Because of who their families were, she might not even have to serve a day in prison.

But what if she tried to get rid of the evidence—and got caught? Murder one. She'd never get out of prison.

John Foster picked up the phone as it rang again. He knew his wife better than she thought. She wouldn't be able to admit guilt, to throw herself on the mercy of the court. The public shame would be too great for her.

No, if Meredith were told that the FBI were not only onto her but also now knew she wasn't pregnant, she would cover her crime. It would just be their word against hers—without the bodies. Delores and Juanita would never talk.

He smiled as he said, "Hello? Is that you, Meredith?" He could see himself on some tropical island. If he sold the house, he could afford a nice boat. He and Meredith had saved enough money that he could live the rest of his life in relative luxury. Without working for his father and father-in-law. Without giving up a dime of his hard-earned money. Without Meredith.

"Meredith, I'm so glad you called."

Chapter Twelve

Hank stayed by the phone. Outside the ranch house, the sky darkened to a soft black velvet. No stars, no moon, no northern lights tonight. Clouds blocked out any light, giving the night an eerie ambiance.

Hank had talked Lucas into staying for a while. They'd made a snack and given up on conversation after a while as they'd waited for the phone to ring.

Lucas hid his nerves well, but Hank could see that the kid really was concerned about Charlotte and the baby—and no doubt beating himself up for leaving her the way he had.

Regret. It wasn't a good way to start a relationship. Hank just hoped to hell the two would get a chance. For the baby's sake if nothing else.

When the call finally came in, he snatched up the phone.

"We've got a GPS reading," the voice on the other end of the line announced.

Meredith had turned on her phone, gotten service and made a call.

As Hank wrote down the longitude and latitude of

where Meredith's call had originated, he glanced over at the map he had spread out on the table.

"Who'd she call?" he asked.

"The John Foster residence."

He found the location on the map. Arlene was right. Meredith hadn't taken Charlotte to Billings or anywhere near it. He hung up and found the spot where Meredith had made a call to her husband just moments before.

Was it where she was holding Charlotte? Or had she been forced to drive somewhere to get cell phone service?

According to the topographical map, there was nothing but open country where the call had come from.

Hank looked up at Lucas. "Do you know that area?"

"Hell, yeah," the biker said studying the map. "I can take you right to it."

That was what Hank had been hoping the kid would say.

The problem was how to get there. "According to this map, there aren't any roads into that country."

"There are roads. Well, trails. You just have to know how to find them."

"How far?" Hank asked.

"Twenty-five, thirty miles. Rough road. We could go there on my bike."

Not a chance. "Draw me a map."

Lucas straightened, met Hank's gaze and shook his head. "You won't be able to find it without me. Trust me. Especially in the dark."

He didn't know whether to believe Lucas or not. But clearly he wasn't going anywhere without the kid.

"Okay," Hank said. "Let me call Arlene." He stepped

into his office and dialed her number. She answered on the fourth ring. "Arlene, I think I've found Charlotte. I'm on my way there. Lucas is going to take me." He heard the rumble of the bike outside the ranch house and swore. "Gotta go." He hung up and raced toward the living room.

Damn kid was planning to take things into his own hands. Hank grabbed the keys and the map off the table and raced outside to his SUV. He could make out the tail-lights on the motorbike. He started the engine and went after him, promising himself he'd kick the kid's butt when he caught him.

Lucas was cooking down the highway, but Hank wasn't about to let him out of his sight. The SUV had a big gas-hog of an engine, and right now Hank was damned glad of it.

The night was bottom-of-a-well black, clouds low, stars nonexistent. The only thing he could see was the white line of the highway in his headlights. No one else was on the road tonight but him and Lucas. Nothing unusual about that in this part of Montana, even in early summer.

This was austere country, wild, open and rolling. The only thing breaking the distant horizon was the purple outline of the Little Rockies. The sky was immense. Only a few trees appeared out of the darkness, huddled around a creek bed or a small pond.

Hank had the feeling that he could keep driving forever and never reach the other horizon.

Ahead, Lucas braked, the light on the back of the bike brightening as he slowed to turn off the highway. They were headed into the country to the south of Whitehorse known as the Breaks. Hank had driven some of the bad-lands. Miles and miles of isolated country and only a few roads, most impassible when wet. Fortunately there hadn't been a rain for days.

He swung onto the dirt road and took off after Lucas. He could barely make out the bike's taillights for the dust the kid was kicking up.

Hank was swearing when his cell phone rang. "Yeah?"

"Thought you'd want to know. She made another call, then a third call, this one from a different location. We have a second reading on her."

He felt around until he found a pen, then in the light of the dashboard he wrote down the new reading on the edge of the map. No way could he check the map and keep up with Lucas. "How far is that from where she made the first call?"

"About fifteen miles."

Meredith must have taken off right after making the call. What the hell?

"She called an Arlene Evans from the first location after calling John Foster. Then she called John Foster from the second location a few minutes ago."

Hank disconnected and speed-dialed Arlene's number. "Arlene!"

"Meredith called," Arlene cried.

"Tell me—" The T in the road came up too fast. He dropped the phone as he had to brake hard, gripping the steering wheel with both hands, and still he barely made the turn. The dust wasn't quite as bad on this more narrow road. He could make out the bike's taillights from a farther distance.

Groping on the floor, he found the cell phone. "Arlene? Sorry, I had to drop the phone. Tell me exactly what Meredith said."

He heard Arlene pull herself together. "She said that if I wanted to see Charlotte or the baby, I was to tell you to back off. She still thinks you're FBI."

"Okay. That's good."

"Hank…" Arlene's voice broke. "I could hear Charlotte in the background. She's in labor!"

That meant that Charlotte had been at the first location that Meredith called from. The one that Lucas was rushing toward right now. But why would Meredith leave with Charlotte in labor? Had she gone to get help? Or was she making a run for it?

"Arlene, I need you to do something for me. Do you have a map of the area?"

"Yes."

"Get it." He waited, driving at a little slower clip, but keeping the bike's lights in sight.

"I have it." Her voice was growing more distant. He was about to lose service.

"I need you to check this longitude and latitude and tell me where it puts you, okay?" He held what he'd written up in the dash light and read it off to her. "Can you find it on your map? Try to hurry. I'm afraid I'm going to lose you." Silence.

Then Arlene's voice, tight, scared. "Hank, if I'm reading this map right, she's headed right for—"

"Arlene? *Arlene?*" He swore and tried to redial, but the no-service signal came up. Disgusted, he tossed the phone on the seat next to him and concentrated on his driving. From what he could tell, they were now about twenty miles south of Whitehorse. He could make out the jagged dark edge of the pines that marked the Missouri Breaks.

After the most recent ice age, the Missouri River changed course, flowing along the southernmost edge of the glaciers, cutting a gorge a thousand feet deep on its way to the Mississippi.

Ahead, Lucas made another turn, slowing down, obviously realizing he wasn't going to lose him. Then suddenly, almost before Hank could react, the bike stopped in a flare of brake lights.

Hank braked, coming to a dust-boiling halt. He jumped out of the SUV and had Lucas by the throat before the punk could get off his bike. Out of the corner of his eye he saw what had stopped Lucas. Someone had felled a huge old cottonwood across the road—and recently.

"What the hell did you think you were doing?" Hank demanded.

"I lost my head," Lucas croaked. "I wanted to be the one to save her. I *needed* to be the one."

Hank gave the kid a shove. He stumbled backward. "That was stupid. Had you found her and gone busting in, you could have gotten her killed." He shook his head, wishing he didn't understand Lucas's reasoning so well. Lucas wanted to make up for the past. Didn't they all? "I'm actually trained in this sort of thing. So trust me, okay?"

Lucas nodded.

"Is there another way?"

He shrugged. "All these ridges lead to the reservoir. We just take the next one over. We'll have to backtrack—"

"Leave your bike," Hank snapped as Lucas started for it. "You're coming with me. One way or the other."

Lucas eyed him in the glow of the SUV's headlights,

clearly not liking taking orders. But maybe he also saw that Hank was in no mood to argue. "Okay."

Hank could have told the kid that he'd be waiting in the SUV once they reached their destination. He had a pair of handcuffs in the glove box and would make sure of it. But right now he just needed Lucas to show him where to go.

They backtracked a mile or so up the road, then took what looked more like a trail.

Hank sensed rather than saw the movement out of the corner of his eye. His gaze shot to the rearview mirror.

He almost ran off the road as he found himself looking into Rena's green eyes—and the dark barrel of the weapon she held trained on him. She hadn't been in the back this whole time. That meant she'd followed them and had gotten into the SUV while he'd been arguing with Lucas.

Hank swore under his breath. He hadn't even thought to look for a tail. Especially someone driving without headlights on.

"Where are we going?" Rena asked, sounding amused as Lucas let out a surprised curse. "Tell your biker friend to be cool."

"Do as she says," Hank said as Rena pressed the barrel of the gun into the back of Lucas's neck.

Rena knew him too well. He would have tried to disarm her if the gun had been on him any longer. But he wouldn't chance it with Lucas.

"There's a young woman," Hank said. "Eighteen, she's having a baby and being held by a desperate woman who wants her baby and her dead. I'm on my way to try to save them both."

Rena cocked a brow and smiled at him in the rearview

mirror. "You always were such a champion of the underdog. By all means, let's go save the girl."

ARLENE HAD LOST HANK. Frantically she tried to reach him again on the cell phone, needing to tell him that according to her map—

She felt the hot breeze skitter across the kitchen floor and realized someone had just opened the front door and was now standing in the doorway.

Bo? She'd gotten into an argument with him when she'd come in to answer the phone, and he'd left, walking down the road, calling someone on his cell phone to no doubt come get him.

So when she turned toward the open front door, she was curious why he would have come back. She'd figured he would be gone for the night.

But it wasn't Bo standing in the open doorway, and she felt her heart leap to her throat as she saw Meredith Foster—and the gun she was holding. She looked very different—no longer pregnant, dressed in jeans, a T-shirt, a jean jacket and sneakers, her hair messed and no makeup.

All Arlene could think was that the coordinates had been right. Meredith had called her just a few miles from here.

"Is anyone else in the house?" Meredith asked.

Arlene shook her head. "Where is my daughter?"

"She needs you."

"I know she's in labor. Is there someone—"

"Yes, now stop wasting time. Let's go." Meredith waved the gun in the direction of the door.

"You're taking me to her?"

"Why else would I be here?"

That was the question Arlene was asking herself. "Is something wrong with Charlotte? The baby? You're here because I need to call the doctor—"

"No." Meredith shook her head impatiently. "Delores and her sister are with her. They have delivered hundreds of babies in Mexico. They assure me she and the baby are doing fine."

Arlene looked from the gun to the woman, trying to make sense of what the woman was here for. Not to take her to Charlotte, Arlene feared. "I don't understand."

"Your daughter needs you. There is nothing more to understand. She's in labor. She's screaming for her mother."

Just the thought of Charlotte screaming for her made Arlene move quickly to the door. A part of her still didn't believe Meredith was taking her to her daughter. But if there was even a chance... She hurried out to the silver SUV parked outside, still running.

"You drive," Meredith ordered.

"You don't have to hold that gun on me," Arlene said as she climbed behind the wheel and Meredith slid into the passenger seat.

Meredith gave her a tight smile as Arlene shifted the SUV into gear and backed out of the yard. "Turn right," Meredith ordered, still holding the gun on her. "It's about fifteen miles from here."

Fifteen miles on this road would put them in the middle of nowhere in the Breaks.

MEREDITH COULDN'T believe how good it felt not to be wearing that stupid maternity form. She pitied pregnant women everywhere, waddling around, eating lunch off their protruding tummies like snack trays.

Arlene Evans hadn't even blinked an eye when she'd seen her without the form. So what John had told her was true. That bastard. Apparently everyone knew what Meredith Foster had done. Or if they didn't, they would soon.

She let out a silent oath under her breath as she rehashed her upsetting phone conversations with her husband. This was all his fault, and he was acting as if there was something wrong with *her?*

Well, it wasn't over yet.

She'd been underestimated her entire life. Had she been born a man, she would have been running her father's and father-in-law's company. Instead she'd had to marry John. As if he would ever be able to take over the business.

Just the thought of John made her cringe. He'd told her that the FBI knew everything, knew that she wasn't pregnant, knew that she'd taken Charlotte Evans, and they were closing in on her. Unless she got rid of all the evidence…

It was the excitement she'd heard in his voice. She'd never been able to elicit any excitement from the son of a bitch. Until now.

"Imagine the newspapers," John said. "They'll have a field day. You'll never be able to show your face in this town again."

Oh, she really did wish she didn't know him so well. "They'll never catch me. I covered my tracks too well," she'd told him.

"So you killed that girl and her baby. You're going to fry," John had said, sounding both horrified and delighted.

"Montana state doesn't 'fry' people, John," she'd said

sarcastically. "They hang them. And they have never hanged a woman." At least that she knew of.

"Then you're going to spend the rest of your natural life in prison." He'd sounded just as thrilled by *that* thought. "I'm putting the house up for sale. I'm buying a boat and sailing around the world."

"John? Are you drunk?"

"Not yet, but I'm thinking about it," he'd said with a laugh. "You've made my life miserable for years, Meredith, but that's over now. I'm free of you. The FBI will catch you. I'll tell them what you told me. Even if they can't find that poor girl's body—"

She'd hung up on him, too angry to even speak. Why she'd called him back, she had no idea.

"Meredith, is that you calling for bail money?" he'd said with a laugh when he'd answered the second time. "I'm sorry, but I can't in good conscience allow someone like you back out on the streets."

He'd definitely been drinking. Celebrating.

She'd hung up without a word. Which wasn't like her.

Neither was changing her plans. John wouldn't expect that. Once she had a plan, she stuck to it come hell or high water. He would expect her to panic. To do something stupid that would if not get her killed at least get her caught. Wouldn't he be surprised that she'd changed her plans at the last minute?

Clearly she wasn't herself.

Chapter Thirteen

The narrow road ran along the sharp backbone of a rocky ridge, erosion eating away at its edges, which dropped precariously down vertical coulees thick with giant scrub juniper and tangled copses of cedar.

Hank had never been on a road more remote or desolate. He half expected a chunk of the earth to break off and drop away, taking them with it. He was beginning to think that Lucas didn't have a clue where they were—let alone that this was a back road to the location they'd been given. Charlotte couldn't be out here.

He did his best to ignore the fact that a hired killer was in the backseat holding a gun on Lucas. He had to concentrate on driving. But his mind reeled. What did Rena have planned? Clearly she could have killed him back down the road. But she wanted something more. Him to suffer? The people around him to suffer? Thank God Arlene wasn't with him—and she would have been if he'd had his way. He'd wanted her near, thinking he could comfort her, protect her.

As the road started to fall way toward the river bottom, he caught the dim light of a house in the distance.

Lucas must have seen it, too. Hank could almost hear the young man's mind at work. The kid was going to do something stupid. Lucas was young, already had regrets when it came to Charlotte. And he was a fearless kid who Hank figured didn't always consider the consequences.

Hank wanted to warn Lucas not to do whatever it was he was thinking of doing, but he didn't dare call attention to the kid. It would only give Rena the edge when Lucas ignored whatever he said and did whatever crazy thing he had in mind.

As they topped a small rise, Hank heard a soft click. Before either he or Rena could react, the passenger-side door swung open and Lucas threw himself out, disappearing over the edge of the road to drop into darkness and nothingness down a steep ravine.

The SUV couldn't have been going more than ten miles an hour at the time because of the road. The kid fell off the backbone of the ridge. If the fall didn't kill him, Rena sure as hell would.

Hank had hit the gas the moment he heard the click of the door opening, throwing Rena off balance. She got off one shot, the boom inside the SUV drowning out most of her expletive.

In his business, Hank had learned to never pass up an opportunity, especially one when it looked as if things were going to hell in a handbasket. Gas pedal to the floor, he jerked the wheel toward the drop-off to the right, grabbed his door handle and bailed.

He knew Rena would anticipate the move. She did. She got off another shot. As he hit the hard ground, tumbling head over heels down the steep slope, he felt a searing pain in his side. But that pain was quickly forgotten as he careened downward through a thick stand of junipers, the limbs scraping, scratching and jabbing as he continue to plummet down the coulee.

In the distance he heard something large crashing through timber. His SUV.

Hank finally managed to grab a limb and stop falling through the blackness of the coulee. He lay for a moment, assessing the damage. The fall had tweaked his left shoulder and left him feeling beaten to hell.

But it was his side that had him most concerned. Although the bullet apparently hadn't hit any vital organs, he'd lost quite a bit of blood. Bracing his feet against the base of one of the larger juniper trees, he took off his long-sleeved shirt, folded it and pressed it to his wound under this T-shirt.

That was the best he could do for the moment. Glancing back up the coulee, he could make out the line of the road above him, the sky a smidgen lighter above it.

He hadn't fallen as far as he'd thought. Which was good, since it was going to be difficult climbing back up. Using the branches of the junipers and small cedars, he began to climb. He wondered where Lucas was. He hoped to hell the kid hadn't broken his fool neck.

At least Lucas had been dressed in all leather. He probably hadn't gotten as scraped up as Hank, blamed kid.

But it was Rena who Hank worried about as he topped the ridge. The road was empty. He listened, heard nothing human. He could see the light of the house just down the road.

He hesitated only a moment. He knew by following the open road down to the house he would be a sitting duck. But he had little choice given the terrain—and the ticking clock.

MEREDITH HAD ARLENE turn off the road onto a trail atop a ridge. Arlene had hunted some of this country with her father when she was younger, before her mother insisted she was too old for such foolishness. Hunters had made most of the roads trying to get to the Breaks, where there were elk, deer and antelope.

If she wasn't wrong, this one was called the Middle Eighth Ridge on a topographical, but it was hard to tell. They all looked the same on a dark night. And it wasn't as if there were signs out here. If you couldn't read a map, you were lost.

Obviously Meredith could read a map.

The road switchbacked down a steep hill, and Arlene caught sight of water—a huge surface of dull silver. Fort Peck Reservoir, with a shoreline that was longer than the entire California coast.

Arlene felt her heart drop. Meredith wasn't taking her to Charlotte. She was driving her out here to kill her. It would be months before some bow hunter found what was left of her remains. Animals would carry off most of the bones. After the vultures picked them clean.

Arlene glanced over at Meredith, thinking she would see this woman in hell first.

"Watch where you're going!" Meredith snapped as Arlene hit a rut in the road, jarring them both as the SUV came down hard, the gun in her hand never wavering.

"You'd better hope my daughter and the baby are all right," Arlene said, gripping the wheel tighter. "And that you're really taking me to her."

"Don't make threats you can't back up," Meredith said

with disinterest. "I've taken good care of your daughter and her unborn baby."

"You can't possibly think you can still get away with passing this baby off as your own," Arlene said.

Just then she saw a light ahead in the distance. Was it possible Meredith had been telling the truth? She could make out a small log building. One of those hunting camps used during the season. Closed the rest of the year. Completely isolated.

The only thing Arlene could think was that no one would hear Charlotte's cries. Or her own.

"Watch out!" Meredith bellowed.

Out of the corner of her eye Arlene saw a large dark figure lurch up onto the road. She hit the brakes as a body careened off the right front of Meredith's fancy SUV and disappeared over the side of the road, into the darkness.

"Keep going," Meredith ordered, shoving the barrel of the gun into her side hard enough to make Arlene gasp.

"But we just hit someone," Arlene snapped.

"Drive. Think of your daughter."

Sick to her stomach, Arlene put the SUV into first gear. The vehicle lurched forward.

Who had she just hit? She couldn't believe someone else was out here. Her heart began to pound. Oh, God, what if it was Hank?

"Stop here," Meredith ordered as they reached a wide spot.

Arlene could see the log structure in the distance. If Charlotte was in there and they were this close…

"Stop!" Meredith ordered, jabbing her again with the gun barrel. "Now get out. You can walk from here."

She couldn't see any vehicles. Just an outside light. Arlene feared Meredith would shoot her once she stepped from the vehicle, but what choice did she have? If there was even a chance that Charlotte was down there…

She put the SUV into Park, pulled up the emergency brake and, unsnapping her seat belt, climbed out.

Meredith quickly slid over behind the wheel and, without another look, turned the SUV around and took off back the way they'd come.

Confused, Arlene looked up the road they'd come down, thinking of the person she'd hit.

A blood-curdling scream rose from the darkness below her. Charlotte. Arlene took off running toward the sound.

HANK HEARD THE scream. He was almost to the lit building, all his senses on alert. He'd seen where his SUV had left the road, the tracks in the soft earth, the bright-skinned bark of the closest juniper. But it was too dark to tell where the SUV had finally landed. Or if Rena had gotten out before it crashed over the side.

He stopped. The whine of a vehicle engine carried on the breeze, and he thought he saw lights through the trees on another ridge in the distance. But the lights were headed in the opposite direction. Someone leaving?

He quickened his pace. The loss of blood made him feel light-headed. He pressed his now-soaked shirt to his side and kept moving.

A small log cabin came into view, rising up out of the darkness and trees. It sat precariously on the edge of the Breaks, overlooking Fort Peck Reservoir, the dull dark sky reflected in the water far below. A dense copse of ponderosa pines flanked the building on three sides.

Hank headed for the trees, weapon in hand. A breeze stirred the pine boughs, making them emit a low, mournful moan. A few stars broke free of the clouds. Silence settled around him.

He didn't know where Lucas had gone, and that worried him. Nor could he see Rena.

He hadn't gone far when he saw the red minivan parked in the pines. No sign of Meredith Foster's silver SUV, though, he noted with concern. Was that who he'd seen driving away?

Hank was to the cabin when he felt the presence in the darkness. An instant later the cold steel of the barrel was pressed to his back. He froze.

"You know how this has to end," Rena said quietly behind him. Her voice held no emotion, but she seemed to be breathing hard, and he suspected she'd been injured. That would only make her more dangerous—if that was possible.

"So what are you waiting for? Shoot me. End it." A breeze stirred the pines nearby, a whisper in the dark. He could smell dust from the vehicle that had left and the unmistakable scent of water close by.

In the distance a flock of geese made an inky ebony vee across the night sky, their soft honks barely audible over the thud of his heart in his ears.

Hadn't he always known this was how it would end for him? Just a few more feet, though, and he would have been inside the cabin. He could hear Charlotte's screams of pain. He felt his gut clench with fear for Charlotte and her baby. His pain was about to end. But hers...

ARLENE WAS ALMOST to the cabin when she caught movement by the door. While she couldn't make out any more than the shapes of two people, she could almost feel the tension in the night air. She slipped into the shadow of the building and held her breath.

One of the figures spoke. A woman, her voice low, sounding almost pained. But it was the second figure's voice that sent a chill skittering up her spine. Hank. So that hadn't been him on the road.

Her relief was short-lived as his words registered. He'd just told the woman to kill him.

Rena? The woman Hank had told her about?

Arlene's eyes had adjusted to the darkness enough that she could make out a woodpile behind her against the side of the building. She eased back to it, quietly lifting one of the more manageable logs into her hands, then she worked her way along the side of the building to the corner again.

The sound of her movements was hidden by her daughter's cries of pain inside the cabin. With each, Arlene felt her heart break. Charlotte was still in labor, having a rough time of it. Arlene desperately needed to reach her daughter's side.

The only thing blocking her way was a hired killer.

"This is between you and me," Hank was saying. "I don't want anyone else hurt."

"You and me?" The woman let out a humorless laugh. "There is no you and me. Not anymore."

"You went to the other side," Hank said. "You knew the price. You knew who would be coming after you."

"Indeed, I did. That is why I'm still alive."

"Rena…"

Arlene didn't dare wait a moment longer. She rounded the corner quickly, the log clutched tightly in both hands as she swung at the smaller figure.

The woman sensed her at the last moment—but not quickly enough.

HANK HAD SEEN ARLENE come down the hill. He'd desperately wanted to cry out a warning for her to go back, but he knew her better than that. She had to get to her daughter. And Arlene wasn't one to back down just because the going had gotten rough.

He reacted the moment she made her move. He spun around, going for the gun, knowing that Rena would have heard the movement behind her. That she would be half turned.

There was a flare of light, an ear-splitting boom and a shower of splinters as the bullet tore through the log in Arlene's hands. But the shot didn't slow down Arlene's swing. The log struck Rena, knocking her into the side of the cabin.

Inside the house came an instant of silence, followed by Charlotte's screams.

The second boom followed swiftly behind the first. This time the shot went wild because Hank was on Rena, fighting for the gun. The third shot was muffled, followed by a groan, then silence.

Hank didn't realize he was all that was holding Rena up until she let go of the gun. Those amazing green eyes of hers met his gaze. She smiled, nodding slightly, as she dropped to her knees, blood blossoming from her chest and streaming down her face from a head wound she must have gotten when she'd jumped from the SUV before it went over the ridge.

She fell to her side, and he saw that the head wound wasn't her only injury. There was a jagged tear in her leg that showed bone. He knew that revenge had been the only thing keeping her standing those last few minutes of her life.

Hank moved quickly to shield Arlene from the corpse, looping an arm around her as he opened the cabin door and, stepping through, drew her in after him. He could feel his side, knew it was bleeding again. He fought the light-headedness. Just a little longer…

ARLENE COULD HEAR Charlotte as Hank ushered her inside the cabin, making sure there was no one waiting to ambush them. The first room was empty. Charlotte's cries were coming from down a short hallway. A light bled out onto the floor from an open doorway.

Arlene practically launched herself at the light. Hank tried to keep in front of her, but her need to reach her daughter was suddenly so urgent, so primal….

She could hear the soft, encouraging murmur of voices in between Charlotte's moans and cries of pain.

As she and Hank reached the doorway, he motioned for her to wait. It was the hardest thing she'd ever done, but rationally she knew what they did in the next few minutes could be a matter of life and death.

One look at his face as he peered into the room and all reason left her. She rounded the edge of the doorway to find two Hispanic women, one at the foot of the bed and the other at the head, near Charlotte.

Arlene had been prepared to see her daughter tied to a bed. Held at gunpoint. Or worse.

Instead the room had been prepared much like a hospital room. Charlotte was propped up, her feet splayed. Delores, the younger of the Hispanic women, was holding the girl's hand, offering words of support in her broken English. She looked up as Arlene entered the room but didn't seem surprised to see her.

"She's my daughter," Arlene said as she rushed to Charlotte's bedside.

The other Hispanic woman at the end of the bed gave her and Hank only a glance and went back to what she'd been doing.

"I'm here," Arlene said as Charlotte burst into tears.

"Mama!" she cried. "Mama."

Arlene hugged her daughter. "It's okay, baby," she said, smoothing back Charlotte's long blond hair from her damp face.

The older woman snapped something in Spanish. Delores translated, "She needs to push with the next contraction."

Arlene nodded and turned to her daughter. "You can do this."

Charlotte was crying and shaking her head. "You have to get me to a hospital. Something is wrong."

"Listen to me," Arlene said, taking her daughter's face in her hands. "Women have given birth for centuries. In the middle of fields. In the backs of cars. This woman knows what she's doing. It will be over soon. You have to do as she says."

Charlotte's sobs lessened as another contraction began, making her suck in her breath.

"Push," Arlene ordered. She glanced toward the woman at the foot of the bed, hoping Meredith had been right. That there wasn't anything wrong. That these women knew what they were doing. Because it was too late, the hospital too far away. Getting a doctor here was out of the question.

"You're doing great," Arlene said to her daughter as Charlotte let out a pained breath and sagged back on the bed.

Delores translated again from the older woman. "She must push very hard at the next contraction."

Arlene nodded. "You did great, Charlotte. It won't be long now."

Her daughter actually smiled at that. Charlotte looked older but none the worse for wear. Apparently Meredith had taken good care of her.

Another contraction seized her and she bent forward, gripping Arlene's hand as she pushed.

The woman at the end of the bed said something in Spanish.

"What?" Arlene demanded.

"She can see the baby's head."

Everything happened quickly after that. Arlene was only vaguely aware of Hank in the room. Or that at some point Lucas had come in looking scraped up and limping. Arlene didn't put it together that he'd been the person she'd clipped with Meredith's SUV. She didn't question what he was doing here or how he'd gotten here or where he'd been. Her only thoughts were with her daughter.

Arlene concentrated on her daughter, feeling each pain as intensely as Charlotte did.

And suddenly, at the end of a long contraction, the baby was expelled. Hank, she saw, had stepped forward to offer his assistance, grabbing some clean towels piled on a table next to the bed.

The older woman gently laid the infant into the thick white towels that Hank held out to her, while the younger woman worked to bind off the cord.

As the baby began to cry, an angry full-lunged howl, Arlene finally let herself feel. Like the baby, she began to cry. Charlotte, exhausted, had tears in her eyes, as well, as she lay back in the bed.

The women took the baby from Hank to clean it up as the infant squalled. Then they handed the baby, wrapped in a clean blanket, to Hank.

He looked down at the baby, smiling as he stepped around the end of the bed to where Arlene stood.

"Would you like to hold your grandson?" he asked.

She nodded and he put the wriggling, crying baby into her arms.

Charlotte sat up to look at her son for a moment, a look of wonder in her gaze.

It was only then that anyone noticed Lucas. At some point in the delivery he'd keeled over.

As he came to on the floor, he said, "It really is a boy?"

That's when Arlene noticed the blood. "Oh, God, Hank, you're hurt."

Chapter Fourteen

At daylight, the emergency room at the Whitehorse hospital was bursting at the seams, between the injured patients, the newborn baby and her mother and the local sheriff's department.

"I'm going to need a statement from both of you," Sheriff Carter Jackson told Hank and Arlene.

The two Hispanic women had been taken into custody, and an APB had been put out on Meredith Foster. Both Hank and Arlene asked for clemency for the Hispanic women.

"If it wasn't for them..." Arlene said, her emotions to close to the edge.

"I understand," the sheriff said. "Arlene, I want to apologize. I'm sorry I didn't take your concerns more seriously."

"It's all right," she said, no doubt surprising him. The old Arlene Evans would be threatening to sue the department and everyone in sight. "Charlotte and the baby are fine. That's all that matters."

The sheriff still looked upset with himself.

"Aren't you getting married in a few hours?" Arlene asked. "Isn't today the Fourth of July?"

He frowned. "Yes, but I—"

"I'm sure your deputy can handle this," she said. "You should go get ready for your wedding. We're all fine."

Lucas had a few cuts and bruises. Even being clipped by Meredith's SUV hadn't been any worse than some of his motorcycle accidents, he said.

Arlene liked watching him with the baby and Charlotte. Maybe there was hope for Lucas yet. Maybe there was hope for all of them.

The gunshot Hank had taken hadn't hit any vital organs, and while he'd lost a lot of blood, the doctor said he was in great shape for his age—didn't she know it—and that he should be up and around in no time. He'd have to recuperate for a while, though.

"Don't worry, I'll take care of him," Arlene told the doctor, then looked over at Hank. "That is, if you'll let me."

He shook his head. "I want to take care of *you*. You saved my life, Arlene."

She brushed that off. "We're even then. You saved mine in more ways than you can imagine. Not to mention that if it hadn't been for you…" Her voice broke. "I don't know what would have happened to Charlotte and my grandson. But all that aside, I'm going to take care of you as long as you need me."

HANK SMILED AND pulled her to him for a kiss. He'd seen a lot of things in his life, but he'd never seen a baby born before.

It had done something to him that he could hardly comprehend. All he knew was that he'd glimpsed his future in the birth of that baby. A future of grandchildren, long horseback rides across the prairie. And maybe someday he and Arlene would travel the world as he'd originally planned. Or maybe they would just sit on the porch and watch the sunset and count their blessings that they'd been given a second chance for happiness.

All of that would have to wait, though. Until he was on his feet again. And then he'd have to take it slow. Arlene would have a lot to adjust to with helping Charlotte plan a wedding and spending time with her new grandson.

But he felt they had all the time in the world now.

Hank had put in a call to one of the numbers he'd told himself he'd forgotten. He'd given the person who answered the information about Rena and the coordinates, and by the time the sheriff's department had reached the cabin, all evidence of Rena was gone. To all accounts, she'd never existed.

He'd told the sheriff that he must have shot himself when he'd taken a fall. Lucas was smarter than he looked. He'd backed up Hank's story of losing control of the SUV on the road.

Rena was dead. That part of his life was truly over.

Arlene finally talked the sheriff into leaving to get ready for his wedding, which was taking place at the Whitehorse Community Center this afternoon, followed by a fireworks show.

"You should go to the wedding," Hank told Arlene.

"I'm not leaving you. The doctor's going to admit you to the hospital. Charlotte has a room down the hall. The doctor said she's sleeping peacefully. She's going to be all right. This has changed her, Hank. She knows now how her lies led to what happened. I'm just so thankful that Meredith took good care of her, probably made her eat better than I was ever able to."

"And the baby?"

"At the nursery. That's where Lucas is. He's so young to be a father, but he's determined to make a life for the three of them. He's already lined up a job on a ranch near here."

"You don't have to stay with me," Hank said. "Don't you have cookies to bake for the fair? A wedding to go to? A fireworks show? A grandson to gaze at?"

Arlene laughed, took his hand and smiled down at him. "I'm right where I want to be."

It wasn't until later that day that they heard Meredith Foster had been arrested. She'd given herself up and had made a full confession—including the murder of her husband John.

In her statement, according to what the deputy told them, Meredith said that unlike pretending to be pregnant, shooting her husband had actually been pleasurable.

"She could have gotten off easy on the other charges," the deputy said. "After all, she took Arlene to her daughter and she made sure there was someone there to deliver the baby. But cold-blooded premeditated murder?" He shook his head. "You got to wonder what she was thinking, huh?"

THE WHITEHORSE Community Center was overflowing. Everyone in several counties had shown up for what they were all calling "the wedding of the century"—the marriage of Eve Bailey and Sheriff Carter Jackson.

If it happened.

Bets were being taken at the local bars.

Even Eve Bailey's sisters weren't too sure.

"Would you stop eyeing me like that," Eve snapped. "I'm *fine*."

"Of course you are," her sister McKenna said, giving their youngest sister, Faith, a wink. "If you were any more fine, we'd have to peel you off the wall."

"I *love* Carter," Eve said. "I'm *marrying* him. *Today*. And nothing is going to stop that from happening. I heard what happened down by the Breaks. But Carter will be here."

McKenna and Faith exchanged looks behind her back.

"I saw that," Eve said and pointed to the large mirror against her bedroom wall. The two laughed and plopped down on their sister's bed.

"It's all going to come off without a hitch," McKenna assured her. "Carter wouldn't miss this. Wild horses couldn't keep him away."

Eve clearly wasn't convinced. "Even if he's late…"

Just then they heard the sirens and all raced to the second-floor window. They could see all the cars parked for a good half mile around the community center—and a cloud of dust coming up the road toward Old Town.

The siren died off as the patrol car skidded to a stop in front of the center. A cheer went up. Eve began to cry. "It's Carter. He made it."

"Of course he did," McKenna said as she and Faith hugged their sister.

"The Whitehorse Sewing Circle decorated the center with fresh flowers," Faith said. "It really is gorgeous."

"What about the food for the reception?" Eve asked, excited and nervous and anxious.

"Laci and Bridger have it covered," McKenna told her.

"I hate to have my brother have to work on the day of my wedding," Eve said, frowning.

"You know Bridger wasn't about to let anyone else cater this wedding," Faith said. "It's his present to you. Don't you think we should get down to the center?"

"Yes," their mother said from the doorway. Lila Bailey Jackson wore an emerald jewel-tone dress that was stunning on her. "May I speak to Eve alone for a moment?" she asked her other two daughters. "We'll meet you at the community center in the bride's room in a few minutes."

"If this is going to be that mother-daughter talk you've been putting off," Eve joked. "It's a few years too late."

Lila smiled and shook her head. "There is nothing I can tell you about life that you haven't already figured out for yourself. There's someone downstairs who needs to talk to you."

Eve felt her heart leap to her throat as she let her mother lead her downstairs to where Pearl Cavanaugh sat in her wheelchair in the kitchen. Eve's twin brother, Bridger, stood at the window. He turned as she walked in.

"I wanted to give you your wedding present early," Pearl said, her speech slow from her stroke but clear enough that Eve had no trouble understanding her.

Eve saw what the woman held on her lap and frowned. Pearl held Eve's quilted baby blanket, the tiny quilt the Whitehorse Sewing Circle had made for her when she was born—just as the women had done for all newborns in the area.

Only her birth hadn't been here. She and her twin brother had never known where they were born. They had each followed the thread of their lives to this spot, Old Town Whitehorse. The rest of the answers had been lost. All they knew is that they were two of the babies who were found homes through an illegal adoption ring run by the women of the Whitehorse Sewing Circle.

"I don't understand," Eve said as she glanced at Bridger. She saw that his quilt was neatly folded in a plastic bag on the table, as it no doubt had been done by his mother for safekeeping.

She met his gaze and saw that he had brought it but didn't seem to understand any more than she did. For months the two of them had been trying to find out who their birth mother was and the circumstances of their birth.

"I told myself that it was best to leave the past where it was," Pearl said. "But the two of you made me see how badly you needed to know about your birth parents." She nodded toward the quilt in Eve's hands. "The answer is in the stitching." Pearl stopped, out of breath.

Eve stared down at the quilt in her hands. The answer is in the stitching? She saw it then, the tiny flowers, each carefully stitched along the border. "The files we found. Flowers. That's the—"

"Key to the code," her twin brother answered for her as he picked up his own quilt, drawing it from the plastic bag to cradle it in his hands. Each quilt apparently had a different flower that matched up with the records the doctor had kept.

Eve met her brother's gaze across the table, tears springing to both their eyes. They both moved to Pearl as one.

"Thank you," Eve said, leaning down to press a kiss to the older woman's smooth cheek.

Bridger took Pearl's hand, and she was smiling her lopsided smile up at him. The two had become close over the last few months, closer than Eve had imagined.

"The truth comes with its own burden, though," Pearl said. "I have kept the secret all these years. But I'm old and I realize I can't let it die with me. So I am passing it to the two of you. Others will come to you over time, seeking the same answers you have. You will have to decide when to share the secret—or if keeping it would be kinder. It is a heavy burden, one I am glad to be free of."

Eve thought of her sisters. Like her, they were adopted. Would they one day change their minds and want to know about their birth mother?

"I trust the two of you to make those decisions in the future," Pearl said. "I guess I knew this day would come when I had the women stitch in a different flower border on each quilt."

The church bell at the community center began to ring.

"Don't you have a wedding to get to?" Pearl asked Eve, smiling up at her.

Eve nodded. "Thank you. You don't know how much this means to me."

"I think I do," she said as Bridger put his quilt back into the plastic bag for safekeeping and placing it in Pearl's lap, pushed her wheelchair toward the door. "I just hope it brings you the peace you so desperately seek."

Epilogue

Arlene hadn't been to the Whitehorse Sewing Circle in months. She'd told herself that she could never hold her head up in that room with those women again. Not after everything that had happened with her family.

That's why she'd sat in her pickup for so long, parked outside the center. Just that morning she'd gotten a call from the state mental hospital. Violet had tried to escape. Her condition seemed to be worsening. The doctor felt she would need more treatment. Violet wouldn't be getting out. At least not for the foreseeable future.

"I think your daughter might be a harm to herself or others at this point," the doctor had said.

"Yes. I wish I had gotten her treatment earlier." As the mother, she should have done something more.

As she got out of the pickup, she prayed it wasn't too late to help Violet and that someday her oldest daughter would be well.

At the Whitehorse Community Center door she hesitated, took a deep breath and pushed, bracing herself as she readied to face down her own demons.

The women around the quilt frame glanced up in surprise as Arlene stepped inside. Just her luck, most of them were here today. Alice Miller, Corky Mathews, Muriel Brown, Ella Cavanaugh, Helene Merchant. Even Pearl Cavanaugh in her wheelchair.

"Hello, Arlene," Pearl said in her slow post-stroke voice. The others murmured their greetings and continued working, sneaking looks at her. "I like your hair that way. It flatters you."

"Thank you, Pearl." Arlene walked across the room and quietly pulled up a chair, several of the women moving aside to give her room to join them around the quilting frame.

Her fingers trembled as she picked up a needle and threaded it. She knew everyone was watching her, but when she looked up, she found them all intent on their sewing.

"Whose quilt are we working on?" she asked after a few moments.

"Your grandson's," Pearl said and smiled a lopsided smile.

Tears stung her eyes. She swallowed the lump in her throat and took a stitch. A comfortable silence seemed to settle over the room.

Arlene remembered when she would have tried to fill the silence with anything she could think to say, usually a bit of gossip she'd heard. Silence had made her nervous.

But today she settled into the work as she made a neat, small stitch on her grandson's quilt, then another one.

Each stitch—even hers—would eventually make up the whole. And for the first time in her life Arlene felt part of something bigger than herself.

THOROUGHBRED LEGACY
The stakes are high when it comes to love,
horse racing, family secrets
and broken promises.

A new exciting Harlequin
continuity series coming soon!
Led by New York Times *bestselling author*
Elizabeth Bevarly
FLIRTING WITH TROUBLE

Here's a preview!

THE DOOR CLOSED behind them, throwing them into darkness and leaving them utterly alone. And the next thing Daniel knew, he heard himself saying, "Marnie, I'm sorry about the way things turned out in Del Mar."

She said nothing at first, only strode across the room and stared out the window beside him. Although he couldn't see her well in the darkness—he still hadn't switched on a light…but then, neither had she—he imagined her expression was a little preoccupied, a little anxious, a little confused.

Finally, very softly, she said, "Are you?"

He nodded, then, worried she wouldn't be able to see the gesture, added, "Yeah. I am. I should have said goodbye to you."

"Yes, you should have."

Actually, he thought, there were a lot of things he should have done in Del Mar. He'd had *a lot* riding on the Pacific Classic, and even more on his entry, Little Joe, but after meeting Marnie, the Pacific Classic had been the last thing on Daniel's mind. His loss at Del Mar had pretty much ended his career before it had even begun, and he'd had to start all over again, rebuilding from nothing.

He simply had not then and did not now have room in his life for a woman as potent as Marnie Roberts. He was a horseman first and foremost. From the time he was a schoolboy, he'd known what he wanted to do with his life—be the best possible trainer he could be.

He had to make sure Marnie understood—and he understood, too—why things had ended the way they had eight years ago. He just wished he could find the words to do that. Hell, he wished he could find the *thoughts* to do that.

"You made me forget things, Marnie, things that I really needed to remember. And that scared the hell out of me. Little Joe should have won the Classic. He was by far the best horse entered in that race. But I didn't give him the attention he needed and deserved that week, because all I could think about was you. Hell, when I woke up that morning all I wanted to do was lie there and look at you, and then wake you up and make love to you again. If I hadn't left when I did—the way I did—I might still be lying there in that bed with you, thinking about nothing else."

"And would that be so terrible?" she asked.

"Of course not," he told her. "But that wasn't why I was in Del Mar," he repeated. "I was in Del Mar to win a race. That was my job. And my work was the most important thing to me."

She said nothing for a moment, only studied his face in the darkness as if looking for the answer to a very important question. Finally she asked, "And what's the most important thing to you now, Daniel?"

Wasn't the answer to that obvious? "My work," he answered automatically.

She nodded slowly. "Of course," she said softly. "That is, after all, what you do best."

Her comment, too, puzzled him. She made it sound as if being good at what he did was a bad thing.

She bit her lip thoughtfully, her eyes fixed on his, glimmering in the scant moonlight that was filtering through the window. And damned if Daniel didn't find himself wanting to pull her into his arms and kiss her. But as much as it might have felt as if no time had passed since Del Mar, there were eight years between now and then. And eight years was a long time in the best of circumstances. For Daniel and Marnie, it was virtually a lifetime.

So Daniel turned and started for the door, then halted. He couldn't just walk away and leave things as they were, unsettled. He'd done that eight years ago and regretted it.

"It *was* good to see you again, Marnie," he said softly. And since he was being honest, he added, "I hope we see each other again."

She didn't say anything in response, only stood silhouetted against the window with her arms wrapped around her in a way that made him wonder whether she was doing it because she was cold, or if she just needed something—someone—to hold on to. In either case, Daniel understood. There was an emptiness clinging to him that he suspected would be there for a long time.

* * * * *

THOROUGHBRED LEGACY
coming soon wherever books are sold!

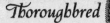

Silhouette
Desire

Royal Seductions

Michelle Celmer delivers a powerful miniseries in
Royal Seductions; where two brothers fight for the
crown and discover love. In *The King's Convenient Bride*,
the king discovers his marriage of convenience to the
woman he's been promised to wed is turning all too
real. The playboy prince proposes a mock engagement
to defuse rumors circulating about him and restore
order to the kingdom…until his pretend fiancée
becomes pregnant in *The Illegitimate Prince's Baby*.

Look for

THE KING'S CONVENIENT BRIDE
&
THE ILLEGITIMATE PRINCE'S BABY

BY MICHELLE CELMER

Available in June 2008 wherever you buy books.

Always Powerful, Passionate and Provocative.

REQUEST YOUR FREE BOOKS!

2 FREE NOVELS
PLUS 2
FREE GIFTS!

◆ HARLEQUIN®
INTRIGUE®

Breathtaking Romantic Suspense

YES! Please send me 2 FREE Harlequin Intrigue® novels and my 2 FREE gifts (gifts are worth about $10). After receiving them, if I don't wish to receive any more books, I can return the shipping statement marked "cancel." If I don't cancel, I will receive 6 brand-new novels every month and be billed just $4.24 per book in the U.S. or $4.99 per book in Canada, plus 25¢ shipping and handling per book and applicable taxes, if any*. That's a savings of close to 15% off the cover price! I understand that accepting the 2 free books and gifts places me under no obligation to buy anything. I can always return a shipment and cancel at any time. Even if I never buy another book from Harlequin, the two free books and gifts are mine to keep forever.

182 HDN EEZ7   382 HDN EEZK

Name	(PLEASE PRINT)

Address		Apt. #

City	State/Prov.	Zip/Postal Code

Signature (if under 18, a parent or guardian must sign)

Mail to the Harlequin Reader Service:
IN U.S.A.: P.O. Box 1867, Buffalo, NY 14240-1867
IN CANADA: P.O. Box 609, Fort Erie, Ontario L2A 5X3

Not valid to current subscribers of Harlequin Intrigue books.

Want to try two free books from another line?
Call 1-800-873-8635 or visit www.morefreebooks.com.

* Terms and prices subject to change without notice. N.Y. residents add applicable sales tax. Canadian residents will be charged applicable provincial taxes and GST. This offer is limited to one order per household. All orders subject to approval. Credit or debit balances in a customer's account(s) may be offset by any other outstanding balance owed by or to the customer. Please allow 4 to 6 weeks for delivery. Offer available while quantities last.

Your Privacy: Harlequin is committed to protecting your privacy. Our Privacy Policy is available online at www.eHarlequin.com or upon request from the Reader Service. From time to time we make our lists of customers available to reputable third parties who may have a product or service of interest to you. If you would prefer we not share your name and address, please check here. ▢

HI08

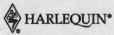